About the Author

Anna String is an author who has written this novella to raise awareness of those living with mental health disorders and seeking a life less ordinary. Her own life has been an interesting one so far. She has spent many years in the consumer research and marketing industry and then transformed her life to be more compatible with her first love, psychology. Creative writing is her passion and her hobby. She hopes to inspire others to share their stories of living with mental health conditions.

Life and Everything Else

Anna String

Life and Everything Else

Olympia Publishers
London

www.olympiapublishers.com
OLYMPIA PAPERBACK EDITION

Copyright © Anna String 2024

The right of Anna String to be identified as author of
this work has been asserted in accordance with sections 77 and 78 of
the Copyright, Designs and Patents Act 1988.

All Rights Reserved

No reproduction, copy or transmission of this publication
may be made without written permission.
No paragraph of this publication may be reproduced,
copied or transmitted save with the written permission of the publisher,
or in accordance with the provisions
of the Copyright Act 1956 (as amended).

Any person who commits any unauthorised act in relation to
this publication may be liable to criminal
prosecution and civil claims for damage.

A CIP catalogue record for this title is
available from the British Library.

ISBN: 978-1-80439-834-0

This is a work of fiction.
Names, characters, places and incidents originate from the writer's
imagination. Any resemblance to actual persons, living or dead, is
purely coincidental.

First Published in 2024

Olympia Publishers
Tallis House
2 Tallis Street
London
EC4Y 0AB

Printed in Great Britain

Dedication

I dedicate this to my godmother, Isabel.

Chapter 1
Family Story

Hello. My name is Hayley. I am going to tell you about my life, and everything else.

Let's start at the beginning. My grandparents' story is one of true love. They met. I am not sure how or where. Possibly at a dance because they both loved dancing and were young and fun. Especially together. My grandfather moved from one city to another to marry my grandmother. She was a gymnast when she was younger. It kept her supple and fit well into her old age. She reached one hundred one years. He reached eighty something. He looked like a Native American man. She was feisty and small. With French and German ancestry. And a wicked sense of humour. She offered her grandchildren chocolate bonbons each time we came to visit from America, South Africa, and Germany itself. Many years later, I discovered there was a chocolate empire in her last name. Unfortunately, the family sold it in 1929, and I was no heir to anything. Other than a pair of opera glasses, an aquamarine stone necklace, and a few other things, like a letter opener.

My grandmother's name was Leah. She lived through two world wars. Her brother died in the second one. So did many other relatives. Their graves are marked in a graveyard so large it requires a bus to navigate through it. It is a beautiful park in a lovely city. A city that was bombed to the ground once. My grandmother spent much of the war learning English. She helped the Americans as soon as they came. My grandfather had been shot in the leg. He had returned home before others. They had rented some fruit trees to be able to live. She looked after someone's children. They told the Nazis to piss off after the war. Many ran away. They were given a space to live with their three children. On the ports of Hamburg. At a ship's wharf where one boy, my uncle, fell in love with ships. He later became an aeronautical engineer in America. My mother immigrated to South Africa. My aunt stayed in Hamburg and became a tax collector. My grandfather worked for a rich man for the rest of his life on the Elbchaussee as a legal and financial aid. A humble but dignified life.

A short note on WW2. Both my grandfathers were stationed on the islands in the north to fight the French and the Allied forces. The one had PTSD after his time in the war. He got away with an injury. The other stayed for longer but also lived. Neither were particularly enthusiastic about the war. They had to go, they had little option about it. The other grandfather had a doctorate in law and opened a bookstore later in his life. His wife helped him to run the shop. They lived in a small village on the Elbe River mouth. The sea goes out far. If you go for a walk on the beach, your toes wriggle in the sand, along with the worms coming out from underneath the earth.

So my mother was born in 1939. An infant at the start of WW2. They were internally displaced people for most of the war. As the middle child, she already had an older brother; the younger sister was on the way. They escaped Hamburg the night before it was bombed out. They had received Intel from my grandfather somehow, so they knew to leave. This little girl spent some nights sleeping around a fireplace in a house full of people who had fled the bombings. They had gone far to the south. Much later, they were at the ports of Hamburg. Thereafter in a small townhouse with a long thin garden out the back. My mother decided to be an adventurer and spend a year abroad. As soon as she could, she sailed on a ship to South Africa. To spend a year learning the English language.

Marianne arrived wearing a coat with a fur lining. Her brown hair rolled into gentle waves. Hello, South Africa! She spent some time in Johannesburg, gallivanting about with some German and Jewish immigrants, in Berea. Somehow she later landed up in Cape Town, where she met my father. Instantly attracted to each other, they soon married. They moved back to Hamburg together but got bored after a year or two. Why not give South Africa another chance? They decided to embark on a great and daring adventure together. They built a house in Llandudno. There was hardly anything there. Elsewhere it was a warzone. South Africa was in the midst of the throes of apartheid or apart hate, as I like to say. They never said anything about it. Not a single word.

My brother was born first. A surfer, a cool kid with ray-bans, and later a dirt bike. His room was full of posters of waves and surfing. Nothing else. He is eight years older than me. The kindest, sweetest person and such a cute kid. He taught me how to ride a bicycle and catch a swing. He went back to Hamburg at eighteen years old. I think my mom shouted at him too much for trying to smoke weed once. Also, he had to do a military service year; it was still compulsory then. He mostly spent his time in an office and learned to be a paramedic. His life has been an interesting one. He partied in Berlin at the fall of the wall in 1989. We had family on both sides. My brother later became a teacher.

I cried when Nelson Mandela was released from prison in

1990. But I had no clue who he was. I never watched television. But this I saw. It got to me. Why didn't I know who this person was? I was only ten. Years later, at my UCT graduation, I stood up with the crowd in Jameson Hall and gave him a standing ovation. I received my undergraduate degree in psychology and gender studies. The honourable chancellor, Graca Machel, and his wife also gave it to me. I was so proud and happy in that moment. I had also been one of the first people to visit Robbeneiland when the prison was still operational. My mom's second husband had some connections by then. We went to look at what we could. We were shown some kind of bunker or military place. Later, I went with my brother and his friends on a regular tour. That time, I saw the prison cells of the political prisoners for the first time.

I forgot to mention that my parents divorced when I was four due to an affair. My father remarried a different woman quite soon. We got along brilliantly and are still friends to this day. She was a woman who loved. She loved everyone. An artist and a visionary. She truly was, and she occupied a special place in my heart. But she said she could never replace my mum, and I always needed to tell my mum how much I loved her. We built homes for fairies in the sand. We painted on silk with paint and wax. We made things with clay.

My aunts also were very special to me as a child. I spent a lot of time with them in Hamburg and in Munich, where they lived. The one loved going to flea markets and finding and collecting strange things. The other one, Lara, made herbal teas and had a garage full of bicycles. We swam naked in the lake, and we rode at dusk when the glow-worms came out in the forest. She pointed out the concentration camp in Dachau but didn't really explain anything. She was a translator and a singer in a church choir. She had those paedo glasses, and she probably hunted some Nazis in her life. Or maybe she just prayed. I don't know. But back to the first aunt, my mother's sister. Isabel was also my godmother from Hamburg. She was a princess. Not really. But really. I will show you her picture.

I went to the German International School in Cape Town. We learned a million things. I loved every minute as a child. As a teenager, I was a bit moody. Buried myself in romance novels and slept in the afternoon. I started horse-riding when I was nine years old. Rode a horse called Flame. My favourite, though, was Golden Ford. Reliable, loving, and kind. My friends also rode. Rebel, the ex-race horse. The unpredictable one. We galloped on the dunes. We did modern dancing too. The James Bond dance. Little did we have a clue as to how the black people had been suffering all the while during apartheid? A war in the minds of many. But I felt loneliness. I felt a sense of where are the people? Wtf am I doing here on my own. Something was wrong.

My father had an arts and crafts factory. Kind of like a craft centre but more like a factory. Because they did everything from the beginning to the end. From design to production and sales. I visited often. Many black women worked there. They barely spoke a word of English. Daphne was the designer of carpets and tapestries. They ended up being incredibly beautiful. Each piece was crafted with so much live and care. The so-called workers should have been paid millions. They were artisans, crafters, creators, and makers of stunning things. Daphne showered them with love every day. She had grown up in what is now Zimbabwe. That's another story.

I was in a homeland once, in Bophuthatswana. Apartheid was happening at that time. I was smuggled through at night to a house, a place where a few ladies wove some tapestries. This place was linked to the business. Not sure how. I think my father must have had permission from the chiefs to be there. At the time, it was the only way possible. When the women met me, they were delighted. They didn't make too much of a big deal of it, but my hair was very white. So I must have looked strange to them. Anyway, I got to weave a small tapestry together with one lady. I still have the piece we made to this day.

Llandudno was my home growing up. So, was Hout Bay later, after my parents' divorce. We moved there, and my mother was a single mom for about ten years. Then, after my brother went back to Hamburg, she met a man. His name was Stephan. He was a grumpy old man who smoked a pipe. I was twelve years old. He was always nice to me, albeit a bit distant. We played cards as a family. Schummeln (cheating). And we all ate ice cream once a week. Stephan listened to pop music on the radio. Always the radio.

I learned later that Stephan had not only worked for the West German government in Bonn for thirty five years in a journalistic capacity in their communications department. He had also spent a considerable amount of his time strategizing militarily and politically. He was interested in security studies and in the department of defence. He even made it his own mission to make friends with some people in Angola and spend two weeks strategizing with them in the bush war. He had been a soldier himself during WW2, a really young one. He was a Catholic with some Jewish ancestry. He also had quite a sense of humour. He had books about WW2, social democracy, the KGB, and the Holocaust. But I wasn't allowed into the study, this was off-limits.

I had my various friends growing up. The German International School was a development school. So there were children of all backgrounds. At least from teenage years. There was a foreign language stream to let in the English kids from a certain grade onward. So it was pretty mixed, which was still a huge deal just after apartheid in South Africa. To me, race is a social construct. It is what it is, but it is also what we make of it.

So my childhood was okay. I was verging between oblivious to subtly in the know. Everything was so obvious in retrospect. But nothing was known to me, not really. Apartheid remained a big mystery. For a long time. My mother sold coffee to various delis. She spent a lot of time driving around. And was always late for picking me up from school. I was the girl waiting on the street corner just outside the school. Always waiting.

In my gap year, I went to London, where I worked in a ceramics café; to Geneva, where I did a French language course; and to Hamburg, where I did an internship in graphic design at a start-up advertising agency. At some point, I realized I would rather study psychology and went back to Cape Town to commence my studies at the University of Cape Town.

When I was in my late twenties and at the beginning of my career in the communications industry, I spent close to two years in Johannesburg. There, I had the opportunity to go to the apartheid museum. I also went on a guided tour of Soweto. I made many friends in the journalism field. I almost met the guys of The Bang Bang Club. They were friends of friends. They would have been horrified at my levels of ignorance and stupidity back then. But a girl has to start somewhere and learn some things the hard way. I had the opportunity to work together with some lovely individuals, however, and together we formed a clique of our own. A kind of new struggle niche. If I may say so myself. Something to take into the future. A hybrid township meets the city kind of future. A future for all.

One of the things that shaped my life the most, aside from friends and family and society, was my work. I had about five jobs in my life, and five years of unemployment. In my first job, I worked for a magazine publisher in marketing and research. In my second job, I was in consumer research and communications testing. In my third job, I worked as a channel strategist at an advertising agency. In my fourth job, I worked as a trend spotter at an international marketing agency. In my fifth job, I worked as a marketing person at a development consultancy. I really enjoyed my work. I loved working with a diverse range of people. My colleagues were great, and the work was interesting.

Anyway, I am at home in Cape Town. But I can make anywhere my home. I usually do so immediately. Wherever I am. My favourite song is "To Build a Home" by the cinematic orchestra. If you play that, you can be at home anywhere.

Chapter 2
The Ancestors

I have been to the Cedarburg mountains a few times. There are original rock art paintings there. It's incredible to think those are drawings made by early San people.

The South Africans, especially the Black South Africans, namely the Tswana, Southern Sotho, Northern Sotho, Xhosa Zulu, Ndebele Venda, Tsonga, and Swati, believe in the ancestors. Their beliefs are that we need to honour and cherish the ancestors, and some of us can connect to their spirits or even become spirit guides. We need to remember, be respectful, and accept their knowing.

In order to honour this and to make my own connections and observations, I started looking at my own ancestry. There is a picture you can draw of your ancestors. Then there is the family tree. Last but not least, there are your living relatives in psychology. You can study family systems and ecosystems too.

My family tree I drew from records given to me by my parents. On the paternal side was a family tree; on the maternal side, we had a story book with many details and stories of different persons and connected families. A bored religious lady had once drawn this up and added in photos as well. So I had plenty of materials to make up my own tree.

Where to begin? My parents' names were Marianne Naeren and Ben Wissen, and my grandparents names were Dr Johannes Wissen and Hanna Ihla, Leah Brand, and Daniel Naeren. My great-grandparents names were Anton Wissen and Lina Primer, Paul Ihla and Marie Fus, Hugo Naeren and Anna Wagner, Philip Brand, and Theresa Wermann. My great great-grandparents were Julian Primer and Katrina Ebert, Matias Fus and Irma Fus, Christoph Naeren and Clara Hartman, Albert Wagner and Janette Kroshevski, Nicolas Wermann, and Anne Sophie Wermann (some missing data on this level). My family tree is on the page. It made me happy to put this together first as notes later on ancestry.com. Many people in the US also practise genealogy. Records of births and deaths can be discovered, among other things. Maybe even living relatives.

I wrote diaries from age twelve to age nineteen. Of course, the best diary ever written is that of Anne Frank. Nothing will ever compare to that. The girl who was, in the end, taken and murdered by Nazis but lived her life in Amsterdam as fully as any child could. I walked past her house. I didn't want to consume it. To enter, it would have been sacrilegious. Before I reached the long queue and ignored it, I saw a black limousine speed past me whilst walking there myself. The man in the limo mock shot me as he was being driven by. It was a warning not to go inside. So I didn't.

The Holocaust (Shoah) happened. It is, to me, the saddest and most tragic event in all of history. That so many millions of people were senselessly murdered is still incomprehensible and beyond belief. But when you look at the hate campaigns and the scapegoating in the propaganda of the Nazis, you can see how it culminated in that. Antisemitism was massive, and it was a dark and dangerous pandemic that gripped the people. It held on to them and consumed them totally. Anyone who wasn't a victim was a perpetrator. People who stayed silent were allowed to live. Dissidents were immediately destroyed. Whilst my grandparents were not a part of the NSDAP or the Nazi Party, they did know others who were. It was an unstoppable energy. Those who tried, like the Scholl siblings, Sophie and Hans of the White Rose student movement, were killed pretty quickly. In 1945, the Soviets liberated those who were still alive in the concentration camps. Thank God for survivors and those who had escaped prior to those times.

So what had happened? The Nazis had held a conference, the Wannsee Conference. About a dozen of them (names are known) had literally planned the Holocaust. This atrocity was then executed, like in some horror movies. It was just the end of the world as anyone had known it. Some of the genociders had even been genocided before. In Namibia, during the colonial period, the Herero, the Nama, and the San were genocided by the Germans then. Germany has since issued an apology and reparations. Many of the perpetrators of prime evil died during or after WW2 themselves. During the Nuremberg trials, some leftover ones were punished more to send a signal that such abuses would never be tolerated ever again, anywhere.

It is a far road from there to find healing and peace within. Many struggle, and many still suffer. And imagine the relatives not yet laid to rest properly. It is a gaping wound in our society that needs to heal. Much is done for the sake of memory, but not enough for healing. As many simply don't know how to recover from this mega event in history.

I walked along the Holocaust Memorial in Berlin. And I saw the Stolpersteine, the Roma Memorial. Sadness reigns supreme. Cape Town has a Holocaust museum and also many individuals who survived the Holocaust. I met one of the survivors on a number of occasions, as one of my friends was his granddaughter. A difficult but important friendship we had. More on that later.

Back to where this chapter began. With the ancestors. In many cultures, people pray to their ancestors. It is crucial for their continued existence and for their very survival. Some ancient cultures perished because their ancestors were unhappy. Or the gods. All cultures need to be in good health to thrive and survive. In Israel today, Judaism is practised, as are other religions. Jerusalem is still the birthplace of religions such as Christianity and Judaism, as well as of major significance to Muslims and others. In Germany, there are many religious sites, and in some cities, there is still much work to be done in the restoration or recreation of many Jewish holy sites and spaces. Synagogues need to be built where they were destroyed during Kristallnacht, the night of broken glass, and elsewhere. Churches and mosques need to be taken care of. Communities need to be re-established, nurtured, and protected. Tolerance should be promoted as people of many different faiths learn to live alongside each other. Because an apology, although valuable, is simply not enough.

Love is the energy required for healing. Also sounds and vibrations. Time might help as well.

Intentions matter. Laicite, or the concept of practising religion at home and in designated spaces, is also useful. In this way, people have space around each other and can live together.

I am learning so much about spirituality and psychology at the moment. There are many connections between the faiths, and once you see them, you can't unsee them. Opening my eyes and my heart was always going to be the way.

As the great granddaughter of a preacher, I can safely say that religion is also truly within me. I haven't told what my ancestors did for a living yet or about their lives. They were mostly at the professional level. Lawyers and engineers, an individual who was a provincial official, a military man, a preacher and a teacher, a fur trader and an ornithologist, a farmer and a bookshop owner, and a kindergarten teacher. The one question I do still have about Leah, however, is whether she might have had some Jewish ancestry as well, somewhere along the line. She definitely had some French lineage. There were French twins in a photo, not sure who they were, but there is some connection there, and I will always be left wondering.

So what does all of this mean?

Whilst it's interesting to think about parents, grandparents, and even great-grandparents, I think at some point, the line is exhausted and doesn't need to be traced further. One of the main reasons is that there is ultimately regeneration in the cells and in how children are made, if you look more closely at the biology of it all. What is the connection between biology and genealogy, then? Perhaps it doesn't make much sense to go beyond the grandparents' level anyway. And so, we are released from our ancestors. Stay liberated, yet informed. And pay attention to the living, relatives, friends, and others! With much love.

May the children be our future. May the ancestors be happy with us, and may the current generation learn to heal. And lead the way.

Also, why did I spend so much time thinking about the ancestors in the first place?

I am a schizaffective person. So schizaffective disorder is a mental disorder characterized by unusual thought processes, an unstable mood, and occasional depression. I have this condition in a mild form. I am through the dark stages and have had psychotic episodes in the past, but I am well and have been stable for a long time. I feel I have a heightened level of consciousness. I am in another place in my life.

I have a hypothesis that schizophrenia could be similar to or linked with the calling by the ancestors to become a traditional healer, also named "go thwasa" in Sesotho or "ukuthwasa" in Isizulu, loosely translated as the calling. At least, if you make it past and beyond a psychotic episode with some guidance, you may have experienced a calling and might pursue the option of helping to heal others. If ignored, it can cause illness or even death. So it is not something to mess with. This info is from a South African psychology textbook, *Understanding Psychopathology: South African Perspectives*. It made me ponder whether I might have experienced a calling to become a healer. This question remains unanswered for now.

Or could I be more like a high priestess? This is associated with spiritual enlightenment and illumination, with calm, wisdom, secrets, and knowledge. It matters that a high priestess goes within to find the path and the way. It has to do with listening and intuition, and connecting to the ether of the universe. And understanding the ancestors is part of that.

Marianne Williamson, in *A Return to Love*, speaks of fears and of a person's light. It is important, she mentions, to let a person's inner light shine, and doing so should not diminish anyone else's light either.

So whether I am potentially a healer or a high priestess remains to be seen.

I will let my light shine.

Chapter 3
Life and DNA

In my life, I have had five boyfriends and three more almost boyfriends. I am going to tell you about those.

My first boyfriend was the beautiful Matt, a cousin of one of my closest friends, Siena. We lost our virginity together. It was a romance across two continents. I was only seventeen. He had curly black hair and olive skin. He was delicious and sexy and yummy and divine. We met again in my gap year and dated for some time. He was the classiest of them all.

In Cape Town, you often meet the same people over and over. My matric dance date, Paul, was one of those people and very special to me. We spent a night together on a farm once. And many others kissing for hours in dodgy clubs we would regularly frequent. Did I mention he was the lead singer of a band. He ran after me one night to get my number. We met again in London, where he lived for many years and met his lovely future wife.

My second boyfriend was Andre. Only for a month, and then I went overseas for a gap year. He was a soccer player, and even my mother said he looked like a god. I left him for London, Hamburg, and Geneva.

In London, I met William, my only black, almost boyfriend. We had a liaison that lasted a few weeks. It started as a professional connection and grew into a mini romance. It involved photography and art, driving on a scooter through

London, and drinking red wine together.

My third boyfriend was Chris. I met him as a student, and he was studying environmental and geographical sciences. We were almost living together. We did a road trip through South Africa, visited Kruger National Park with friends, and even met up in Barcelona, Spain, once. He was the kindest person ever. He could draw like a demon.

My fourth boyfriend was Kian. An Irish name for not being a terrorist. The name means dark, and dark he was. But on the inside. This one liked trance parties and shrooming, had more gay friends than you can imagine, and took me to Verbier, Switzerland, for snowboarding. We also went to Paris, but it was cold and icy, and we didn't really know what to say to each other any more. Then a lot of drama happened, which I won't mention here. He ended up in New York, working in advertising.

With a broken heart and an injured neck, I went off to Johannesburg. There, I guided one of my male friends, called Noam, towards his marriage. If he hadn't had the most wonderful fiancé, I would have snatched him up myself. A stellar wedding, though, and a beautiful marriage ensued for him. We shared many stories, though, and he helped me heal a little.

My fifth boyfriend was Aiden, a man of all men. He was vegan and Buddhist-inspired, a challenger, and a friend. We went camping together and spent a few weekends away. In darling Robertson and in Stanford, amongst other places. He spoke fluent Dutch, and he was slightly Asian-looking. We also spent the weekend on a golf estate with his best friend, Tanaka. The place belonged to his uncle, and it was generous of him to take us there.

My last boyfriend was also my second boyfriend on repeat. He re-entered my life, and he became one of the greatest challenges. He was deep and also slightly autistic, or at least bipolar. An alcoholic of note. Not to be compared to number three, who had at this point become a crack cocaine addict. He is in recovery now. It must be a personality profile. The girl who dates addicts. *Hmm.* I do love them. Sometimes I feel they are the only people who truly 'get' me.

Well, and last but not least, there was Stephane. A French Moroccan guy. Here for not very long, just long enough to get to know him intimately and have a stunning breakfast together.

But back to my personality profile. My profile, according to Persolog profiles, is that of the special advisor. I love giving advice, solicited or not. Beyond being sincere and friendly at the core, I am able to develop harmonious relationships, assist people in planning and organisation, and I like to focus on creating a climate of cooperation. I can become a better-rounded person by confronting others directly, and sharing negative feelings with others. I handle conflict by compromising and proposing a middle ground. This reflects my personal values of knowledge, stability, appreciation, and service. I am motivated by opportunities to satisfy my personal need to exercise completion, belonging, and trust. I respond to pressure by being open to alternatives. That's the essence of my personality.

I am hopeful and optimistic for the future. The thing is this. I think I may have found true love. With number four. The one who got away returned to me as a friend. Perhaps that is all we will ever be. For now, it's plenty. More than enough. I love this person so much that it almost hurts. But it also fills me up with the most immense joy and the deepest sense of calm and gratitude. I think that successful living, like in a Diesel ad (with scooters) and Zen and the art of motorcycle maintenance, those would be the secrets to a marriage.

I am bilingual... But actually, I speak four languages.

Languages are one of my talents. I love playing with languages. In South Africa, there are eleven official languages. We are so lucky to have this linguistic diversity. Speaking more than one language is empowering and increases your neural networks. Also, your ability to communicate with others.

Many organisms on the planet follow energy. Organisms go where there is more energy or higher vibration. A means of communication is to do with reading energy fields. Energy, as we know it, is in fact life.

So I did a DNA test. In a completely unrelated move to any of the above, just to further explore my ancestry. I am feeling somewhat enlightened. I had a couple of questions that needed answering.

Anyway. I am apparently 89% from the Western and Northern European (German, British, and French), 5% of Finnish Origin (Baltic), 5% from the South European (Sardinian and Tuscan origin), and 1% Southeast Asian. The last one came as a bit of a surprise, but I had wondered about it. Now I can compare my family tree to the results. What's also emerging is that I come from many coastal places.

Oh, so fascinating! The results will become even more specific in the future. Aren't many of us from at least four or five groups anyway, some more or less distributed from around the globe? If you think of your total group of ancestors, which shows up in your genetics. It's to do with complexity. All very interesting.

Hmm, so not too sure why I did this test or what I hoped to achieve with it. But I did see two inspiring stories about genetic ancestry.

The first was when Archbishop Desmond Tutu participated

in genetic testing. Little known fact. He discovered he was also a surprise from the Khoisan, amongst others. His hope was that more genetics research would lead to health benefits.

Then I also saw an interview with a Holocaust survivor from the Ashkenazi Jewish who found living relatives through the testing. What a miracle. And what a story.

So all I can say is I am going to sleep on this a little, think about the findings, and I enjoyed learning more about my places of origin.

A word on genetics. It seems to have been proven that we are all related, at least, or derivatives of one another in some ways. Some DNA sequences, for example, are blocked in some individuals and not in others, and hence we look different from one another. There is diversity in humans.

In a country that suffered through apartheid it has massive implications. It's not to bring anyone new categories or new groups. It's more about appreciating a more complex way of looking at things, of accepting mathematical formulas that pretty much determine levels of diversity. This diversity is amazingly enough in each one of us. We are all connected in some way, and getting closer to a better understanding of those connections.

We also live close to the cradle of humankind, which is in Maropeng in South Africa. The out-of-Africa theory of evolution postulates that we all come from Africa. The competing multiregional theory states that we come from many regions. Regardless, we are all bound together by our humanity.

My point is. We connect. To loved ones. To family. To ancestry. Even to present and future generations. We need to value life deeply. We need to care deeply about life, and value life at its very roots.

I woke up to another day and had more thoughts on this DNA stuff.

There are many life and health related questions that can be answered using genetic tests and research. So there are many issues and propensities that can be looked at. I am no expert, though. All I can say is you can explore this further, for example, by reading scientific American or nature magazines.

Many illnesses are inherited. They are in the building blocks, in your genetics. So, for example, schizaffective disorder is located in my DNA. Whether or not it comes out and makes an appearance in a lifetime in part depends on environmental factors. Certain environmental conditions make this condition appear. In my case, many stressors added up and led to psychotic episodes. With therapy and medication, I got back on the right path in life.

Another thought that I had was that there must be renewal in the passing down of the genes. What I am trying to say is that if someone gets in, it probably lasts about maximum of seven generations, and then the genes are out again. And so the gene pool is constantly refreshed. This is just a hypothesis. And whilst we can celebrate our ancestry, we should also look forward to future generations and possibilities.

What implications could this have?

An implication might be to do with the passing down from generation to generation of royal titles. I know it is not only about the lineage, it is also about culture. I am questioning the royal lines of succession. Could there be another way? For example, could royal leaders be elected by a council? Or the people?

Such questions and others have arisen from doing the genetic research, using myself as a sort of test case. My ancestry is mostly north German, from the region of Hamburg. I knew about the French person and the British person in my family tree, and the Italian from Milan as well. So that is all confirmed to be true. And as it turns out, I am partially indigenous to the Baltic region. So I have indigenous and ancestral rights.

Of course, not only the "originals" have rights to a place. Also, anybody who happens to be there. Ranging from other citizens from elsewhere to migrants and travellers. All have rights and should have rights. That is beyond a doubt in my mind.

There is always space and energy for "newbies," as the thinker Phillippe Legrain pointed out in his book on immigrants. We need to start thinking beyond nationalities. It's nice to have one, even two. Currently, our rights are tied to nationalities. There are stateless persons, and they need to be assisted. Then there needs to be more regional and bilateral as well as multilateral agreements amongst, between, and across countries. There could be a more international way of being, could there not?

Limitations and possibilities. It's good to think about these. DNA is the building block that forms the basis of who we are. And what we could be.

I am reminded that it took us about half a year to discover in my physics class at school that light can be both particles and waves at the same time. This is known as wave-particle duality. And so it will be with genetics research, as with any new research, that it will require both time and patience. And flexible minds. As well as scientific rigour. New ideas can be interesting and dangerous. Of course, we should not make false links. As we learn more, we also need to unlearn. Keywords for the future:

Unlearning – co-creating – participating

When will we...

Un-learn?
Un-do?
Un-create?
Un-think?
Re-make?
Re-do?
Re-think?
Re-design?
Co-create?
Co-exist?
Co-imagine?
Co-learn?

Chapter 4
Beliefs

I live in a house that is very meaningful. It is the house of sustainability. It has a church window in the front. It has high ceilings and open beams. French doors leading out to a garden on two levels. A small rockpool at the back. Many ficus trees and beautiful plants, including a white rose bush to commemorate the white rose movement and many clivias and indigenous fynbos plants. The first guest room has a stone wall on the inside, which keeps it cool and reminds me of the inside of a pyramid in Egypt. I have a sacred scarab stone in it, which is a symbol of renewal and rebirth.

The other room has a stained glass door leading into it and a cherry blossom tree decal on the wall from the previous owners, who used it as a baby room. It makes me think of Kyoto in Japan, another sacred place. I am just using it as a study for now. The table and the fireplace both have five line markings on them. I imagined one day that these were the number of people you may kill in a lifetime. If you are a knight. As a knight's honour and all that. In the modern paradigm, perhaps not literally, but figuratively. In the main lounge, I have some art, including a ghostly painting of black horses, a dream or a nightmare, depending on your state of mind, a design poster of Nelson Mandela, a huge photo of an indigenous Masaai guy, and the photo of JFK and Jackie Kennedy on a sailing boat, symbolising my wish for a happy marriage, as well as a William Kentridge poster for the magic flute. I recently bought a lamp, which I absolutely love, as it bathes the room in a gentle warm, white light at night.

Upstairs in the bedroom, I have my wonderful cupboard, with my shoe collection and my precious clothes, all carefully selected and taken care of. I had no clothes growing up; I hardly had anything to wear at all. I can still remember some items I wore, like black and white striped leggings, a California t-shirt, and a lavender jacket, that I was so in love with. I have a unique sense of style that I like to play with. Moreover, upstairs I have a wicker chair with an embroidered cushion. A second fireplace that I haven't used yet. My precious shell collection and rose quartz spheres. These are symbolic stones of unconditional love. My amber necklaces have to do with safe travel and creating a happy space. I love my book collections as well.

As it might be possible to guess, I am a spiritual person. Slightly pagan and also Christian. Although critical but mostly my mind is in a transcendental state at this point in my life. It's also Jewish affected and Buddhist inspired. I will share some of my deepest beliefs and thoughts on religion. Please do not be offended if you hold other beliefs yourself. It is possible to read on with judgment suspended. And to take it all in, as these were some of my sources of inspiration for the chapter to follow.

From the pagan and the Celtic, I take not only sounds and songs but also the meanings to do with protections and eternal love. When two people tell each other that they love each other, they are bound together. This may or may not be true. It depends on their bond and the nature of the connection. True love. It is or it isn't. There is an apple tree symbol that denotes true love. My mum grew up in apple tree country in Hamburg. Where they rented fruit trees. So this connects through to my heritage. Apple trees and orchards are meaningful to me. They speak of land and of love. I also think of the thistle given by the woman wrapped in cloth in "Braveheart." I think of when I used to make rings out of pine tree needles in the garden growing up. And I used to imagine making many healing potions by mixing herbs together from our herb garden. I used to get irritated because nobody could tell me how to mix the potions together. Imagine this as a child.

I have an herb garden now as well as a book on what the herbs mean. I believe in nature's garden and in natural healing. In shamans and in the local complementary medicines. I like that there is a natural remedies shop right next to the pharmacy in town. There is much to say about paganism, and many books are available on the topic. I find it's what you make meaningful and how you make it a part of your life that's important. Most of all, it's about a reverence for nature and an appreciation of all life on earth. But it might mean many things to many people. I have an appreciation and respect for all things Celtic and Nordic, these are closest to my own beliefs.

Then there are indigenous and natural religions. For example, the beliefs of the Native American Indians and the aboriginal people. There is so much to say about these. For the latter, dreaming is important, as are snakes and many other wild animals that hold deep significance. I really don't know that much, but I have at various times looked quite deeply into these beliefs. In the Native American, there are plenty of signs and symbols as well as sacred practises. One such practise I will mention here is healing circles called hocokah in the Lakota language. This is a sacred circle, also another word for altar, and people sit in a circle to talk, pray, and help each other heal.

In South Africa, there are many practises to do with shamanism and indigenous or traditional beliefs. Ranging from the Khoisan to the many cultures, including the Sotho and the Isixhosa, to name just two. There is also a lot of knowledge on differing mental states and respect for people's many possible states of mind. When you have the gift, you may become a shaman or a traditional healer. Isixhosa traditional healers are known as amaxhwele, or herbalists, or as amagqirhs, or diviners. Ngaka and Selaoli are the words in northern and southern Sotho, respectively.

The Christians have kept some pagan traditions, either knowingly or unknowingly too. The Christmas tree is a well-known pagan tradition that was included in the Christian faith. Pagans used fir trees in their homes to symbolise everlasting life and fertility. The tree would be decorated mostly with lights or candles and decorative elements to celebrate the return of light after many dark nights and days.

There are many Christian denominations, and I am mostly familiar with the Catholic and Lutheran variations. And the Anglicans as well. In Catholicism, there is the Holy Trinity, which is the Father, the Holy Spirit, and the Son of Christ. The seven heavenly virtues are chastity, temperance, charity, diligence, patience, kindness, and humility. Their polar opposites are the seven sins. Those include wrath or anger, greed, sloth, pride, lust, envy, and gluttony. I am sure there are a few more. Remembering the Ten Commandments is important to Christians.

I have prayed in all kinds of churches and have been fortunate enough to see many churches, even orthodox ones. The church of spilled blood in St Petersburg is one such place that needs to be mentioned. It is a most phenomenal space. But I also appreciate the simplicity or grandiosity of other places of worship, such as the Rock Church in Helsinki or the St Georges Cathedral in Cape Town. In Hamburg and in Berlin, there are others that were bombed out during the war and rebuilt. Places of worship just make me happy.

I love going into any of them anywhere in the world and feeling a sense of awe and inspiration, or simply remembering to go inside myself and find my inner strength and love for all. I was at a lecture in St Paul's Cathedral in London once in my life. The speech was about the Millennium Development Goals, and it was held by none other than Kofi Annan, the head of the UN at the time. At the time, I didn't know that much about anything also not the UN, but I had always admired them and their work. I ended up working for a while for a development consultancy that had some of the UN bodies as a client's later in life. But these moments in the cathedral inspired me for the rest of my life.

In fact, a day later, I woke up late, and this saved my life. As I wasn't the victim of the terrorist attack that rocked London in 2005. Also known as 7/7. Interestingly enough, 7/7 is also a sign that angels are guiding you. Mine were certainly watching over me that day. Anyway, I woke up, and London had been plunged into chaos. I was only there for two weeks on a holiday, visiting a couple of friends. It is very sad for the victims of those attacks. May they rest in peace. But the thing is, I was literally supposed to be on that train in that subway. I just overslept. A narrow escape. So I can thank my lucky stars. Thank god. Thank the heavens that may be. If I wasn't religious yet, I became one on that day. September 11 in New York was another cataclysmic event that I saw happen on television in 2011. It was a terrible tragedy. There were many heroes on that day, though, and they deserve to be commended for their bravery and fighting spirit.

In the Jewish faith, there are so many meanings and interpretations to name I don't even know where to begin. I am lucky enough to have had various Jewish friends in my life, especially Ava, and to have been invited to certain events, including a lovely Friday night, Shabbat family dinner or two. I think synagogues are beautiful. I am fascinated by the Ten Sefirot, the system of thought behind them, especially. The more mystical side of it is the Kabbalah, which postulates that there are interconnected attributes that describe creation. There are different levels of action thought and emotional levels in any system of thought. The points of interest include kingship, the foundation, majesty, endurance, harmony, judgement, loving, kindness, knowledge, wisdom, understanding, and the crown. I won't claim to know how it works at this point, but I have read *The Anatomy of the Spirit* by Caroline Myss and would refer interested persons to that book for further insights. Only I do get daily devotional insights on my Instagram feed from spiritually inspired accounts as well as from other faiths.

Kwanzaa is a religion that has some crossover with the Jewish faith. Especially in the menorah, the ten candles are similar to the seven candles in Kwaanza. It is, at its core, a festival celebrating African American culture. The principles of Kwanzaa are: Umoja (unity), Kujichagulia (self-determination), Ujima (collective work and responsibility), Ujamaa (cooperative economics), Nia (purpose), Kuumba (creativity), and Imani (faith).

Another book that influenced my thinking was *The Universe in a Single Atom* by Dalai Lama. He was interested in everything as a young child and was characterised by open-mindedness and naturally loving kindness. Of course, he was a dear friend of

Archbishop Desmond Tutu's and together they wrote a book about finding joy. The archbishop is well known for his capacity for forgiveness and for his efforts at reconciliation in South Africa. Also for giving the country the concept of the rainbow nation, that all the diverse peoples might live together in peace. Archbishop Desmond Tutu's book, *Made for Goodness,* is waiting for me on my bookshelf. I am not sure how good I am sometimes. My moral and ethical axes are not that strong. I am more interested in the truth and in finding information, in doing research. Is it science and knowledge we really want? I wonder sometimes.

If you are leaning towards the scientific, then there are, of course, philosophies to support this. One such philosophy is humanism. This philosophy of life says it is our own responsibility to lead ethical lives of personal fulfilment that aspire to the greater good, without theism or supernatural beliefs. It is a commitment to human values and ethical principles.

A belief in the interconnectedness of all life and in the relationships between all of us lies in the South African concept of Ubuntu. This is an ancient African word meaning 'humanity to others'. The sentence 'I am what I am because of who we all are' sums it up beautifully. It demonstrates the essence of this core belief among many people in South Africa and globally as well. Often, it is presented as a more collective approach to living together rather than valuing individualism; it values society as a whole. It is present in everyday life, and it necessitates that people care about each other and look out for each other. People are in fact connected to one another, whether they know it or not.

Some persons can extend their brains and their thoughts beyond themselves in a telepathic manner and literally connect to others minds. This is not known to many. It is another gift.

Another mental gift is that of mind-reading, which some individuals can do. Still different from that is visioning or seeing. Sometimes that means looking deeper into the present, sometimes into the past, and even into future times. Time is another concept to talk about. A thinker on time worth considering is Einstein's lesser-known friend, Gödel. He wrote an essay about time, which is discussed in the book, *A World Without Time: The Forgotten Legacy of Gödel and Einstein*. The latter endorsed the essay and called it an important contribution, especially to the concept of time.

Then, of course, there are more eastern philosophies of thought and belief systems. Ranging from Buddhism to Hinduism to Daoism and many more. I have been to a number of temples in my life, including the temple at Bronkhorstspruit in South Africa, to celebrate the lunar New Year. The lunar calendar provides much guidance and meaning to people. In the western world, many are more familiar with the zodiac, and indeed, there are some similarities there. The Hindus, of course, gave the world Diwali, or the festival of lights, as well as Holi, the festival of colours. In the festival of lights, clay lamps are used and lit outside people's homes to symbolise inner light protecting them from spiritual darkness. I have also been to a Hindu temple in Bali to pray with a local lady who guided me. We had small natural baskets filled with flower petals and burned incense all whilst praying to the gods. This was in Bali, and in Mauritius, I was given a red dot on my forehead, a bindi, which signifies marriage or a wish for everlasting love. An all-seeing eye represents omniscience, or the gateway to the soul. The eye of Providence shows that God watches over humanity.

Last but not least, my first love gave me a protection a red band to wear on my wrist until it falls off. This was from the

Buddhists, and it was meant to absorb negative energy. The Buddhists believe in rebirth and renewal and give people chances. For the Buddhists, the chakras are a source of inspiration to many and the basis of much medical knowledge. The seven chakras represent energy centres in the body and are characterised according to their functions and spiritual meanings.

In fact, many religions have contributed towards people looking after their health and wellbeing. The religion probably best known for its fasting traditions is the Muslim faith. I don't know too much about it, but I do live in a country with some Muslim practising people in it and I have some friends as well. So I am aware of Ramadan and regular praying times at the mosques. There is even an open mosque in Cape Town which welcomes people of all faiths to come and see what the tradition is all about. In Zoroastrism, there is also an epic cosmology of good and evil, with the hope that good wins over evil and prevails. Voudoo is also well known for this and for its purpose of combining traditional African thought and spirits with Roman Catholic elements as well. It has helped many to overcome issues around slavery and oppression and, as such, has always had liberating qualities.

Finally, I would like to mention the book, *A Theory of Everything* by Ken Wilber, an integral thinker pushing the integral agenda. This thinking is based on a schemata of solving real world problems, and it brings closer to home how we can integrate spiritual thought and apply it to our everyday lives. It is totally brilliant and well worth a read. Also Thomas Berry's book on sustainability, *The Great Work,* is a do not miss. It's about love and respect for the planet and its people, the works of God, or whomever you might believe in, if anything.

Of course, I should not forget to mention the atheists. Many moved towards this as they were punished for being religious by their systems or as they moved away from religion in order to be more supportive of specific political systems instead, such as in Russian society for example. Others simply lost their faith or were disillusioned by the many conflicts religions may have inadvertently caused or been party to. It's possible to think of Ireland and the conflicts between the Catholics and the Protestants. Or of Israel, and the ongoing conflicts between those of the Jewish and Muslim faiths. It is sad to see such situations and to feel the damages being done.

I pray for peace and hope for lasting resolutions to any such issues anywhere in the world. There are, of course, many things to think about, also the division between the more formal main religions and the many indigenous belief systems and nature religions. These faiths need more recognition and respect from the established ones. There was a world indigenous people's forum set up by the UN once, but it lost momentum. There are some traditional indigenous peoples that have set up councils of their own, for example, the Sami in Norway and the traditional council in South Africa, which serves a number of groups within. The Native American Indians are part of a growing indigenous people's movement. There is more respect as people are now also elected, e.g., to the senate in the US. And participating in mainstream society. Perhaps mainstreaming is the way to go, not sidelining or creating double structures. But then highlighting that the individuals are also representing a major interest group.

Also, always remember that music gives life, and healing, and replenishes energy. Music is like life. And that could not be truer.

So whatever you believe, whatever your faith or your system of thought, make it count.

Chapter 5
Systems of Thinking

There are many thought systems in this world. In the last chapter, we explored some beliefs, ideas, and ways of being. Schizophrenics and schizaffective persons are particularly good at pattern recognition. And at creating systems. Just saying. We are known for it. And so…

I am going to present a framework for thinking and systems thinking to you. I have named it Visionarie. It is the result of many years of hard work. Whilst it might seem simple at first, its potential is infinite. Please try to understand on a number of levels.

So, what is it? This is my concept note.

The underlying frame and its meaning:
The underlying model is its own version of bringing together all matter and thought.

It encompasses five realms, ranging from the physical to the metaphysical, the relational to the meta-relational, and towards a realisation of the spirit of yourself as you are connected to others. It puts you at the centre of all things as the observer. You are functioning as 'the eye'. But beyond external observations, there are also internal thoughts and feelings that might emerge.

The five realms together form a system. It is a system that is compatible with the physical and the quantum worlds. Perhaps it can go through time if applied correctly. Ultimately, if this model is present in all minds, the multiplier effect will set in. And people could connect in the five realms on different themes.

The themes for exploration and completion:
The shape of the thought system is in a sort of compass network shape that connects the eight themes.

Underlying the themes are all aspects of life. The themes cover various aspects of life, such as mobility, habitation, technology, health, power, systems, development, trade, exchange, education, and more.

Specifically, the themes are: (physical)
Mobility, movement, and home, habitat; (metaphysical) - innovation, tech and health, happiness; (relational) - power, systems, and trade, exchange, education; (meta-relational) - people, development and sustainability, nature.

You in the centre – connecting yourself:

It is for your own personal vision, to shape your dreams, your ideas, to see, influence, and shape the past, present, and future.

You might at first be interested in gathering information and knowledge on the themes, later in seeing how they relate to each other, and also, how your ideas compare to those of others.

Uses and applications and sharing and comparing with others:
A part of the idea is to gather concepts for a vision of the past, the present, and potentially the future. It is based on integrated thinking. This thought system can be used to sort your

thoughts, also to discover gaps or great omissions, areas where you have no knowledge or would like to improve your insights. Thus, looking at your own Intel but also that of others is useful. People should be able to share insights gathered easily. Through simple communication.

In my mind, this thought framework can be used to visualise and co-create as well. It has many uses and applications. It can even be presented with blank circles so that people can think of their own themes and trouble shoot on specific questions and projects. You are welcome to it! Please participate.

"Life is but a dream... Within a dream," said Shakespeare. And this system of thought could help you realise a dream. Some more details to follow.

The frame is therefore:

0 spirit: profile of person/user

Themes:

Physical:

1. Mobility Movement
2. Home Habitation

Metaphysical:

3. Innovation Tech
4. Health Happiness

Relational:

5. Power Systems
6. Trade Exchange Education

Meta-relational:

7. People Development
8. Sustainability Nature

Descriptions

0 spirit: profile of person/user

You are the user. Share a short bio here. Add a profile photo and connect to other users. Share and collaborate on ideas. And special projects. Let your interests and skills guide you. Welcome!

Themes:

Physical:

1. Mobility Movement – Mobility is to do with the ability to move from one place to another; as such, it has to do with transportation and systems of mobility. Movement and migration are also themes. Express your thoughts here.

2. Home Habitation – Home is the structure you live in, whatever type of house it might be. In habitation, we find

many different styles and technologies employed, many plans, and different needs and wants. Architects might love this space, as well as designers of all kinds. Share your designs and ideas.

Metaphysical:

3. Innovation Tech – Innovation is the name of the game for many forward-thinking individuals. Technology often enables this, and it's great to keep up with the latest trends. Make your ideas happen here.

4. Health Happiness – Health is the most important asset you will have in your life. Money might not be able to buy either health or happiness, but anyone can make the decision to be happy. Post what makes you happy!

Relational:

5. Power Systems – Some people are in power, and others are just powerful. Power comes in many shapes and forms. As do systems that can change and adapt all the time. Share your thoughts on power and systems here.

6. Trade Exchange Education – Trade is essential for human survival and has a long history. Its future depends on what we do now, on our exchanges and interactions. There are many possibilities for education. This might bring us into the future. Share your ideas!

Meta-relational:

7. People Development – People are people, we are humans first and foremost, but we also have complex identities. Development is key to create a more equal world and to make life more liveable beyond survival so that all can live well. Contribute to the current thinking here.

8. Sustainability Nature – Sustainability is crucial for the longer term future, also our short term future and present is impacted by this. Nature is a key ally in our survival and presents a challenge as well. Share your thoughts here.

Explanation of underlying themes:

Physical and metaphysical:
Physical things are material things you can grasp and hold on to. Actual stuff with physical properties. For example, a tree, a bicycle, a house, or a person. Metaphysical things are above and beyond the physical world. They could be feelings such as happiness, or intangible things like new ideas that lead to innovation.

Relational and meta-relational
Relational things are between people and include things like connections, networks, and relationships. Meta-relational things are above such relationships and are like systems, for example, in nature and in the greater world out there. They could be complex structures, and it could link to quantum physics ultimately. If anyone understands that let me know.

This thought system is unique and comes in the shape of a

circle, with circles representing the eight themes and the spirit representing point 0 in the middle of the circle. See diagram below for the shape of the system. It could aid anyone with the discovery of ideas, collection of thoughts, comparison of details, and the sharing of concepts.

In the future, I would like to put this online and create a system for people to use. Perhaps my dream will come true, or perhaps not. I hope that with this thought system, people can create next level thinking.

Some more principles of life…

On change and chaos
Chaos in you and chaos in me. All is chaos. All is life.

On sanity and madness
Madness is a blessing in disguise.

On prosperity and dreams
Dream as if you are about to die. Dream as if your spirit is about to lift out of your body. Astral travel and see the world.

On peace and the state of the world
It's never too late to make peace. The world needs it.

On changing the course of history
People have more agency than you might think. Have some faith.

On truth seeking
The truth is not for everybody.

On the light and darkness in all of us

We are light just as we are dark. Integrate those two sides. And you will walk in heaven.

Final thoughts

Love and live life.

Chapter 6
Spirit

What is the spirit? And why is it so critical to understand this? Psychologists and trauma counsellors have been trying to lift people's spirits through the ages. Sometimes we reach our own spirit through dreams and interpretations. Sometimes through transcendental meditation. Many individuals at festivals like Africa Burn are trying to reconnect with the Earth, the planet, and even the people. The stars are often in alignment, for those who are in tune with their spirit. Places have a spirit too, and it can be said that animals do too. The recognition of this in the law is of utmost importance globally, so that animals can realise their full rights and reassume their rightful places alongside the humans on this planet.

South Africa has many special places where there are currents of energy running through that can hardly be described in words. One such sacred space is Hogsback, the eco altar, also in Soweto, there is one there as well. Connecting not only to the ancients, the gods, and the ancestors, but also to actual physical energy centres. Others believe in ley lines, particularly amongst the English and the Nordic peoples. And the African people. Ultimately, spirit is what's within you, your sacred energy.

Oliver Sacks was famously known to have recommended gardening and music to mental patients. As a returning mature psychology student, I also believe that the two things that help the most to restore mental health are gardening and music. The spirit rejuvenates and finds its way back into the body, when listening to beautiful music, deep music, or interesting music. It is food for the soul and nourishment for the spirit.

I hope that people are able to stay connected to their sacred energies and tap into their spirit at any time they choose. Some are more disconnected than others, and then it is up to those around them to try to help them find their way back to themselves. The spirit does not give up easily, the spirit is always there for you. Your spirit is your life force, and it is not alone, it is never alone. There are always spirits around us, guiding, aiding, and helping. Some may see more than others in this regard. It is simply a question of letting go and accepting the energies and currents of the universe. The spirit guides us.

Some further questions. Are we really born free? Is worth considering. In India, for many centuries, the caste system kept people locked into certain professions and positions. Only in the last century has this begun to change, and possibilities have opened up for people to be treated as individuals. Much has changed in India. People are able to choose their professions freely and to pursue an education.

Of course, we can also look at the question through the lens of slavery and the abolition of slavery. The very idea that people were enslaved is horrifying. Almost unimaginable to me. The descendants of slaves I am sure would have a lot to say on this topic, and I would rather hear it from them and listen to their voices come through. In my opinion, we should all be born free and stay free throughout our lives.

Nothing breaks the spirit as much as being abused or being tortured. I am anti-cruelty, if nothing else. Resilience in the face of adversity is brilliant. Although… I prefer reaching a point of vulnerability. Of going far beyond resilience. The latter is what helps to overcome. Without it, many would not survive. It is the greatest weapon we have in our arsenal. Lifting the human spirit out of crisis and elevating ourselves above. Reconnecting with people, networks, and the earth itself. Spirit is in all of us.

But how does the spirit get into us? That remains a mystery. Some believe that we choose this life and our spirit enters the body at an appropriate moment. Not sure when, maybe at birth? That would imply that we have chosen this life, and this life chooses us in return. There are many beliefs about the spirit and the body and their connection to one another.

And naturally, it leads on to the discussion around when the spirit leaves the body. I have a book called "After," and it is about death and the experience of dying. I just haven't had a chance to read it yet. My uncle David has been clinically dead for a minute. His heart stopped. But he came back. His will to live was strong enough. And he just wasn't done with life yet. When the time comes for us to meet our maker (or not, depending on what you believe in), I hope it's an uninterrupted path to heaven. We might even merge with the skies, the earth, and the universe. Whatever happens, I hope for a peace filled end to my life, one day far from today. That it might happen when the time is just right. Timing is everything.

Sadly, both my aunts passed away from cancer, of breast cancer and ovarian cancer, respectively. It was so sad to see them when they were sick, and even more sad when they could not fight off the cancer but succumbed to the illness. Both were in their early fifties. They still visit me in their dreams to this day, as does my grandmother and my mother's late husband, from time to time. I call these dreams visitations. They usually have important things to say to me, messages to relay, and they send me love as well.

Some believe that angels are there to guide and protect us. Faeries, on the other hand, are mythical beings or a form of spirit. They are supernatural creatures. In many cultures, the Fae link our human world with higher powers. They are associated with bringing good fortune, protection, and healing.

Animals have spirits too, and need to be both respected and protected by humans. That is our place in the natural order of things. Many seem to have forgotten this, and this disconnect manifests as pain and suffering. We need to get back to a place of being connected, of contributing to the natural world, as far as we can. Then our spirits will reconnect to the essence, the source, to Gaia.

Gaia is the earth's spirit. It is a Greek word for the name of the earth goddess. I don't know much about ancient history or Greek and Roman times. Except for the difference between Corinthian, Doric, and ionic columns. From the history of art. But Gaia is a concept that we should familiarise ourselves with. It has to do with respect for nature and reverence for the earth. It leads to a transcendental state of mind. This is a great place to be.

Many indigenous cultures are highly interlinked with spirit. The Great Spirit is the idea of a life force. In Lakota, it's called Wakan Tanka. There are many further names for this in first nation cultures. Many rituals and traditions are about the Great Spirit.

Carl Jung spoke of the spirit with great reverence and respect. Several concepts are presented simultaneously by the famous psychoanalyst. He links the earth's spirit to a person's spirit. It is definitely one of the most fascinating and important ideas of our age.

One of the places I found and reconnected with my own

spirit was on the Ilala, travelling up Lake Malawi and sleeping under the stars. This was truly a magical experience.

I am awaiting a global awakening. Some are already there, others are blind, and yet others are refusing to see. I am reminded of the tree in the movie, *Avatar*. The tree of souls is a sacred site for the Na'vi and has a connection to Eywa, the all-mother or guiding force of life. It is a tall tree with bioluminescent tendrils and a large root system. The tree can connect to the human nervous system and heal. Eywa, the great mother, keeps the ecosystem in equilibrium.

There are many sacred and holy sites in Cape Town. The water Camissa is one of these sacred things. Camissa means "sweet water for all" in Kora, the Khoe language of the Cape. It is the name of the river that flows from the mountain (the table mountain) rising from the sea down to the sea. The river system has many tributaries and springs and runs beneath the city today.

This leads me to the topic of neuroplasticity. Neural networks in the brain can grow and regenerate. We have the power to literally change our brains. That is the most empowering and incredible thing. One of the best books I have read is *My Stroke of Insight* by Dr Jill Bolte Taylor. In it, she describes getting back to basic brain functions and retraining her brain after she had experienced a stroke. It is a deeply personal account that demonstrates neuroplasticity in action. It is incredible how much the brain can heal itself.

For regular people, it's possible to benefit from this function of neuroplasticity simply by training your brain. By playing video games, making music, learning a language, practising writing, creating art, actively gardening, exercising, travelling, and being exposed to new ideas. Many ways to keep your spirit alive and kicking.

Another book I am totally dying to read is *Sophie's World* by Jostein Gaarder, as it's about a teenager's exploration of philosophy and life. My most favourite author, though, is Marian Keyes, who has written many books about different female lead characters and their challenges in life. *Rachel's Holiday,* for example, deals with addiction and a stint in rehab with some wit and humanity. I saw her speak once at the Cape Town book fair, and after that, I had to read all of her books. I am a girl obsessed. I loved every single one. Another discovery is Chimamanda Ngozi Adichie and her seminal book, *We Should All Be Feminists.* Which I could not agree more with. Maya Angelou has written many incredible books, including *And Still I Rise.* There is a gratitude journal called *Be present in all things, and thankful for all things,* by her as well. Journaling and opportunities for creative writing are invaluable.

Lastly, for those who are disabled, or have some limitations, like myself, there are often moments that are disheartening or disspiriting. It's crucial to overcome and be firm in the face of obstacles. Be they physical or emotional barriers. The joy of life is simply too important to ever let go of. That too is a part of spirit.

The ability to choose how to respond. To be less reactive and more responsive is important. Viktor Frankl, the author and Holocaust survivor spoke of the ability to choose how to respond. He was an existentialist who wrote about how to have hope in the darkest of times. Out of his own experiences. What is remarkable is his respect for life and the incredible will to survive and live. He formulated a meaning-cantered approach that promotes freedom of choice and emphasises personal responsibility.

This liberates the spirit. I wish you liberty, freedom, and happiness. As Kahlil Gibran said life needs spirit.

In the last two years, the coronavirus pandemic has circled the globe. I am saddened by how many people passed away during this time. Millions of people. It was shocking, and it has left a gaping hole. This global event should be commemorated somehow and kept in our memory. The people should be remembered.

As a schizaffective person, I feel it's very important to stay connected to my inner spirit, my way of being depends on this. I also feel it's crucial to be connected to a higher power, a god, or God himself or herself. Many schizaffective persons go through a religious crisis at one point or another; it's almost a part of the description of the illness. An obsession with faith, with religion, with spirituality, with trying to make sense, and find meaning. Luckily, I have been on my journey, and come out the other side, all the wiser and happier for that. I can only recommend to others to find their own ways, and ameliorate their spirits.

A blessing:

In Spiritus Sancti. May we find the breath of life. In Hebrew, the word for spirit, breath, and wind is "ruach." That is also the original meaning of my name. With spirit.

Chapter 7
Peace and My Mind

When thinking about peace, it is almost impossible not to also think about the dark side of war, conflict, genocide, and other crimes against humanity. I once made a list of all evils and bad things. But I lost it, so readers will just have to use their imaginations and their own dark forces, whatever they may be.

Most importantly, in the mid-1960s, there was a big worldwide awakening and peace movement in light of the Vietnam War. Many who didn't want to join the armed forces and serve in the military because they didn't believe in the war simply refused. We are seeing the same even today as protests in Russia flare up and thousands escape the draught by fleeing the country. Others were not so lucky and were drafted by force into the war against Ukraine. A country that simply wanted to maintain its independence.

I am thankful to all those who have fought for liberty, for justice, for freedom and for all things good and true. War veterans often experience symptoms of trauma and PTSD. There are new ways to overcome this, and with special thanks to any testers of drugs that made this possible. I would like to suggest alternative routes, such as micro-dosing of psilocybin, a compound found in fungi or mushrooms. In some places, such substances are legal; in other places, they are not, so please adhere to the laws in whatever country you are in. But know this, hope is at hand. These substances are currently being developed into medicines that will be available for use in the future. So there is hope.

I myself have experienced many mental states. I have little experience with drugs, having only ever tried hashish once, smoked week twice, and taken mushrooms the same amount of times. But those were moments of joy and enlightenment. The world was glittery and sparkly, and happy for me. Transformed into a beautiful, surreal place that held only wonder and possibilities.

Also, I have gone over to the dark side and had two psychotic episodes in my life. Where my mind was in overdrive and also at last shut down. In any event, I have also experienced severe depression once or twice. I do not really know what caused me to tip over into a psychotic state. These episodes were preceded by creative times, but I could not catch myself and slid into a dark place. In the first episode, I was overwhelmed and confused by too much input and external stimulation from the greater world out there, as well as a series of unusual and inexplicable events occurring.

In the second episode, I was experiencing rage as a result of certain points of focus, namely the Holocaust and subsequent expulsions of the Germans from Königsberg. A place my grandfather was originally from and that his father had been partially responsible for as a provincial official, so somehow I got a bit confused and took on too much responsibility. When, in fact, that is shared. But I do accept partial blame and responsibility for all things that happened and have made my family history as war vets known. So there is some guilt, and I would like to say on their and my own behalf that we are deeply sorry. In fact, I was institutionalised for six weeks after running around in my own garden screaming at the top of my lungs. I was medicated and have been responsibly dosing myself (on psychiatrists instructions) with antipsychotics ever since. I was diagnosed with schizaffective disorder. The medication do work, although there are some unpleasant side effects, but they're all manageable.

But here is some background on the shocking historical events I was referring to.

The museum of Jewish heritage in New York and the Holocaust Centre in Cape Town tell the story of the Holocaust, where six million people died in concentration camps in Europe during the Nazi period under national socialism. They were mostly from minority groups, including the Jewish, the Roma, the mental, the disabled, the dissidents, LGBTQIA+ persons, and more people. This part of history is incredibly tragic and should never be forgotten, nor should something like this ever happen again.

The documentation centre in Berlin speaks also of the subsequent expulsions of Germans, both civilian and formerly Nazi, from Eastern Europe and the north in what is now Kalinska. About 12 to 14 million people were forced to move and go westwards towards modern day Germany. At least, 600,000 people died on the move, if not many more. This too is a tragic period in history and shows how a people who did wrong were punished for their crimes. Of course, this region fell to Russia after the war, which is still contentious at best.

Germany, or what was left of it, was split into east and west and occupied by the Americans and the Russians. The French and the English soon left, realising that they were their neighbours who had to live together in the future. The Americans had a more distant, and more professional, less emotional approach and were able to deal with the Germans. In my family, we had persons on both sides. It's still difficult to reconnect with those who were on the other side though, even years after reunification, especially because the Russians drummed the concept of the family out of them and put in place a reverence for the state instead. However, some resisted and secretly or openly made the best of their own lives.

What still needs to happen is further reconciliation between the Germans and the rest of the world. It is difficult in the present time as the greatest wish is for world peace, which is currently not the case. In the meantime, at least let me apologise again to the British, the Americans, the French, the Russians in particular, all the allied forces globally, and the axis forces as well. For WW2 and any role my family may have played in that. My deepest sympathy for anyone who lost anyone during WW2.

So it is with this in mind. That I share with you the poem below.

A wish for global love and change

I wish for you

Niainan beings > to resonate
The pagan > to be and to exist
The other religious > to guide
The liberated people > to be happy
The diverse ones > to rise
The loved > to give to others

The various Christian followers > to think
Those of the Jewish faith > to heal

The spiritual people > to learn
The LGBTQIA+ persons > to connect
The hopeful ones > to stay with hope
The sad > to be granted a wish
The Muslim religion > to accept
And the Buddhist practice > to meditate
The atheists > to study and to believe
The scared > to be less fearful
The emotional ones > to be stable
The sacred > to be valued

And the Black people > to act
The historically disadvantaged > to be advantaged
The political > to listen and to act
The musical ones > to play
The historical > to inform
The leaders > to talk

The German speaking people > to live
The Italian speaking people > to speak up
The parents > to love
The children > to discover
The truth-seekers > to find
The hopeful ones > to be rewarded

Also the French speaking people > to forgive
The English speaking people > to feel
The talented > to create
The joyful > to be resilient
The whisperers > to be heard
And all beings > to be open

The Southern Africans > to connect
The collectives > to be artisan
The interest groups > to be interesting
The individuals > to exist
The troublemakers > to breathe
The protestors > to care

The Zimbabweans > to thrive
The Ethiopians > to make peace
The stolen from > to be given back
The protected > to be self-driven
The freed > to be happy
The emancipated > to be spirited

Many Russian individuals > to be free
The Ukrainian persons > to change
And all others > to disarm
The respected > to protect
The fighters > to live and to go
The returned > to make

Then the people of Israel > to exist
The Palestinians > to grow
The integrated > to be tolerant
The different ones > to find common ground
The conflicted > to find peace
The absolved > to share

The people of the Far East > to live

The individuals in Myanmar > to get up
The people of Tibet > to meditate
The transcendent > to deliver
The healed ones > to share and to return to self
The learned > to pass on wisdom

And the Chinese people > to act
The Japanese people > to find the way
The harmony seekers > to love
The travellers > to find and to explore
The true love ones > to last
The single ones > to look for love and life

Then the Brazilians > to balance
The Venezuelans > to find a path
The spirits and ancestors > to rest and to guide
The mental ones > to heal and be well
The future > to happen
And the past > to make way

Those in the Congo > to heal
And in Rwanda > to love
The global agenda > to reach goals
Climate change activists > to be heard
The poor ones > to overcome
The rich elsewhere > to give back

Then the US people > to unpolarise
The learned > to unlearn
The slave owners descendants > to reparate
The makers > to co-create

The writers > to elaborate
The doers > to do something great

And the women and men in Iran > to live
As well as in Afghanistan > to learn
The spirited people > to fight on
The individuals > to exist
The brave ones > to continue
The resistors > to survive

Those in Egypt > to hear
The people in Jordan > to take note
The poetic > to write down
The singers > to share
The performers > to liven things up
The disabled ones > to get a chance

The UK individuals > to have a say
And those in India > to celebrate
The married > to forgive
The happy > to impart learnings
The many travellers > to leave no trace
And the cultural ones > to be eclectic

A good night of all nights

Now I am ready to share with you what it was like for me.

My schizaffective diagnosis probably saved my life. At least it altered its course irrevocably. I am now compelled to disclose to those close to me that I live with this condition. It makes me different and unique. Some people chose distance, and yet others affirmed their connection. Mostly those who are also slightly mad or mental. I have some bipolar friends, know other schizophrenic individuals, and some addicts and previously eating disordered persons. It's mental health mayhem in my world. Not to forget about the mildly depressives and the obsessive compulsives. Those with narcissistic personality disorder are not really my cup of tea, or are they? I don't know. It all depends. But I am also friends with apparently sane people. I like to make exceptions.

During my time at an institute, I made a few more friends. There was Bridget, the girl with ginger hair. There was Annette, the lady with the makeup bag. There was Victoria, the woman with braids, and an exercise complex. We were an eclectic lot. I survived. I was frustrated and could not believe I had landed in this place. I was sad about it. I was also on a lot of medication. So I slept a lot. As the six weeks went by, I participated in an art class and a drumming circle. My mother came to visit me often. One friend was brave enough to do the same and visited me once. The doctors annoyed me. They should have been my friends, not people who kept me locked in this strange place. Well, anyway. Most of all, I missed my cat. Routines were established. Days went by. It was a long wait.

But the healing process was in its initial stages. At first, more damage than good was done. The humiliation of being in an institute was something I could not overcome. It was absolute hate for me. I have been suddenly stripped of all my rights. For no reason. It's a very dehumanising experience. The movie "*Girl,*

Interrupted," with actresses Winona Ryder and Angelina Jolie, paints a pretty accurate picture of what it's like to be in an institute for a while.

I wrote later to the police complaints unit. They had brought me to the hospital. I received no response. I wrote to the South African Human Rights Commission. They said they were not that interested, and the matter happened long ago. At least, they took note. I hope they will be able to create a better legal environment for mental health in the future.

I looked at the laws in South Africa, and they leave much to be desired. The focus is not on wellbeing but rather on the state's right to detain the mentally. What an insanity and an oversight. I hope mental health activists can change this. A positive attitude towards mental health is required. I like the NGO MindFreedom International. They are against forced institutionalisations. I agree with that, yet I do believe in mental health care. A forced approach has the potential to ruin lives. A participatory and consenting approach probably has better outcomes for both patients and society as a whole.

Subsequent to the life-altering institutionalisation, I experienced some discrimination at work. After revealing to human resources that I was on medication for a mental health condition, I was asked to sign a new contract stipulating that I did not have a mental health condition. That was the harsh reality I had to face. It was a difficult situation to be in. At another place of work, I dared to take a mental health day. And handed in a sick note signed by my psychiatrist. That was accepted without any questions. I realised that I could not push the boundaries too much, but rather had to live with the level of understanding that society had at the time.

I also want to thank my best friends, who supported me unconditionally. I want to thank all mental health activists. And mental health professionals. For their ongoing support and understanding. Especially the British royals and television personalities like Oprah, who have done much to highlight mental health issues and raise awareness.

Whilst I couldn't get a "sane" declaration from anyone, I did manage to tackle the illness and get through it. It's just that it's a chronic condition that is (as is currently understood) with you for life. Only my comprehension of it is that it's temporary and that it's possible to get through it and come out the other side. And to experience the world in new ways. I think it's open for debate. Most professionals think it's too risky to let people go off their medications though. As they want to avoid a reoccurrence, and the focus is on staying well. And living. So I will stay a part of the 1% of schizaffective people. I choose to be medicated and to live a balanced life.

There are many types of thought. They include what? That is interest based thinking (political right), who? That is identity politics (political left), where? That is location based thinking (geographical and spiritual), when? That is time based ideas (philosophical), why? That is explanations-based thinking (academic), how? That is technical based thought and design (professional). I think I find myself most often on a spiritual level.

As I make peace in my mind and with myself, so I can make peace with others also. I hope others are able to do the same.

Be a mensch, be a person.

On the mental and mind freedom.

Your mind is yours.
Keep it safe. Keep it sound.

Your mind has potential.
Let it grow. Let it develop.

Your mind is generous.
Let it generate. Let it reach further.

Your mind is adventurous.
Be prepared. It will take you places.

Your mind is shareable.
Let it connect. Let it network.

Your mind is sacred.
Care for it. Enjoy it.

Your mind is fun.
Let it be playful. Let it experiment.

Your mind is free.
Keep it liberated. Be open.

Your mind is love.
Keep it kind. Keep it gentle.

Your mind is power.
Let it participate. Let it lead.

Your mind is creative.
Stay artistic. Be available to others.

Your mind is problem solving.
Let it be numerical. Work things out.

Your mind is a great gift.
Be unique. Be together.

Chapter 8
Interdependence

What I want is a new global order. One that allows for peace but also for life and for people to get what they want. For bad regimes not to flourish but rather for the people and good leadership to thrive.

So on the basis of all of those historical events mentioned in the last chapter and my personal links to them, I started imagining. What if my grandfather hadn't left Königsberg before the war? What if they had moved there instead of to Hamburg? Bad, terrible, and shocking things happened in Hamburg too, like the Neuengamme concentration camp. And the rest of WW2, with the bombing out of the city. But would he have been able to avert any greater disasters in what became Kalinska? The simple answer is: not on his own.

Would it have been possible to avoid WW2 at all? To have stopped and turned the tide. Some people say yes. But it is still sad because it didn't happen. And so friends and family, our English and French counterparts, as well as the Russians, bore the brunt of German aggression, not to forget to mention the Polish and the rest of the world ultimately. Only Italy, Japan, and some others sided with Nazi Germany, as they had their own dark forces of, for example, fascism to deal with. What a disaster it all was.

I thought further and thought, *Would it be possible to liberate Kalinska and start over?* This is but a dream and one that cannot be realised in the current global context. But I thought... What if... we had independence for Kalinska? And called it something else, like Niaina?

Of course, there are independence movements to learn from in history with great leaders such as Patrice Lumumba in the Congo. He was assassinated, sadly. He wanted to liberate the Congo and ensure it was run by the Congolese and not by Belgium. Another good example is the recent breakaway of South Sudan from Sudan and how a new country has been established. It shows there is room for change. But people have to fight for that.

This random place, Kalinska, thus became a space for my imagination to run wild. A great place to dream about. The Russians provide a lot of inspiration on Instagram. It's easy to fall in love with the place. After all, my great grandparents were from Tranßau, now Ozerov, close to the Straits. But hey, the others were from Hamburg, and that too is a place for me to dream of, and one I can actually go to, and where I still have family today. Only the problem with Kalinska is that now it's become a military base for the Russians as well, with nuclear weapons sitting there, waiting. I am against nuclear weapons. Hiroshima and Nagasaki were disasters of note. Also Pearl Harbour. All these events need to be understood in an integrated fashion.

So I am not that happy with what became of my ancestral place. What with WW2, the Holocaust, the Soviet takeover, and the continued Russian aggression towards the west. But I will continue to use the place as a springboard for ideas. Because somehow I am connected to its energy. I can't explain, but somehow it's in me. In my dreams of the straits, my thoughts of wandering the promenade by the sea, my ideas of sitting in the forest, doing forest bathing, and finding odd pieces of amber lying around. It's in the animals in the forest and the people in the parks and the inner city. It's love, actually.

So I imagined what if this place were Niaina. Or Niaina were the place of nowhere. Then I said I am on the council for Niaina (as my great grandfather was). A council of ten. Presided over by a king and queen. Chosen by the council, who were suggested by the people. Kind of like a senate running the show. I just imagined all of these things. Perhaps it's to do with a yearning for good leadership. And a place of my own. Although I do believe you can make any place a place called home. So I took that and made it global. A global supernode you can zoom into. It's a bit sci-fi a bit Star Wars. The Niainans are the people from this node. And why not?

And at the end of the day, I realised there is only one thing higher than independence. And that is interdependence. But in order for interdependence to happen, a place first needs to exist.

So here's my concept note.

Manifesto

Niaina is the place of nowhere, a global supernode. It is open to hybrids of all kinds, to beings of light and wonder, who seek and find joy in the world, and practise kindness, compassion, and respect for life. Please see the agenda at the house below and the poem.

Niaina, the place of nowhere
Or my imaginary global supernode
(which may or may not exist at some point in the future)

Agenda at this house (Niaina)

Human growth and development psychology
Sustainability and climate change, e.g.
Equality and liberty gender and women's studies
Communication and self-expression art
Spirituality and religions in moderation
Anti-racism and advancement of black people
Peace building and anti-war efforts
Interdependence and interconnectedness
Family, fun, and the pursuit of happiness
Trauma counselling and life purpose
Freedom of association and liberty
Power balanced with love
Anti-poverty towards prosperity
Financial empowerment and equitable
Distribution and opportunities for all
Lifelong learning, travel, and cultures
Animal rights and spirit soul awakenings
Children's happiness, safety, and education
Nature and wild animal's spaces in balance
Tech, innovation, and insight
Health, wellness, and movement body
Food and sustenance: no meat
Chaos theory and physics
Pagan and natural systems and beliefs
Indigenous rights and values
Philosophy, politics, and psychology

Economics and history
Futures thinking
Humanism

A poem for Niaina

Niaina, the place of nowhere
Filled with imagination and love

I am one of the council of ten for life
We are one for all, and all for one

We are responsible for 27 million people
We are with faith, love, and courage
Humility, charity, and kindness
And we are responsible for the survival of the planet
With passion and harnessing the forces of fire, air, water, earth, and ether
Acting for the wild and the animals on this earth
In their best interests

I pledge this oath
Of faithfulness and servitude
Of acting with love always
And staying open to others
Being with compassion and diplomacy

Wild and free
With liberty, freedom, humanity, and equality
Walking through with resilience
And staying with vulnerability

Elegance and grace

Amen and love to you
From the way of nowhere
And all Niainans
From our liberated global node to yours
Be Fae be free

Niaina

#iamniainan #niaina #past #heritage #present #future #council #power #withlove #heritageday #love #founder #foundingprinciples #country #independence #interdependence #global #node #supernode #superpower #momentum #manifestation #existence #being #random #moments #life #good #endofwars #startoffreedom #freedom #liberty #vulnerability #kindness #balance #people #planet #flow #beyond #spirit #truelove #infinity #nowhere #nowhereland #way #thewayofnowhere #illumination #path #pathways #development #anatomical #neuralnetworks #nextlevelthinking #levels #challenges #resolutions #thoughtstarters #peace #love #light #grace #fairness #virtues #landscape #heaven #heart #Internal #communication #seeing #artofseeing #wayoflife

A prayer

Niaina, my imaginary dream country is going global. It will be a supernode. Like all movements. Small but beautiful. Fair and true. Woven in between all places. Anywhere and everywhere. A home for the homeless. A voice for the voiceless. Hope for those who need to find their way. A place in their hearts. Space. Freedom. Independence from strange, lost leaders of the times. A way of life. A way of being. If you are Niainan, you will know it. You will be called on to make a difference. Develop your potential. Be brilliant. Your best possible self. It is with human development. The preservation of wildlife and our planet. Sweeping forces of change are upon us. Only Niainans will make it through. Praying for all. Praying for the future. We are beyond passports, beyond places, and beyond even ourselves. We are with the forces of life. Unstoppable beings. Filled with spirit and awesomeness. We are one. We are interconnected through the intangibles. We will rise. Let us exist, let us be, let us live, we whisper. And the whispers grow louder until they sound like the wind. The elemental forces shape us and act for us. The forces are growing and linking together. A movement for life, for those who have been oppressed, been damaged, or hurt. No more. Enough is enough. We are beyond it all. The present energies will mingle, filter, and rise. Storms are upon us. Let us play and rediscover our powers as we awaken to our full forces of being. Healing, loving, and living our fullest lives. May peace be with us.

Amen. Bless all Niainans.

Concept note
For the kingdom or global node of Niaina

The king and queen, or rulers
Nominated and installed

Population
27 million

Space or location
Global nodes in cities and other places

Council in power
10 rotating persons

Age or time
New, ancient, and present moments

Stage
Evolutionary phase III

Food or sustenance
Vegetarian pescatarian fruitarian poultrarian

Rights or laws
Constitution with ongoing changes

Sense of belonging
Signifiers like the three dots triangle circle square

Values
Purpose, growth, truth, love, wealth, and authenticity

Sounds or music
Anything and nature driven

Natural world
Many wild animals and indigenous people

Energy
Whatever it is in the future

Status
At peace in transition

Missions
Varied personal and timeous

Look or feel
Anything, including elemental futuristic fashion
Home
Communications dependant

Beliefs systems
Hybrid variations religious indigenous cool

Humans
Diverse random sampling trends

Predictions or ideas
Past, present, and future paths

Currency or trade
Gifts trade exchange money digital hybrid

Collections or ownership
Personal owners and safe keepers of things

Secrets and quiet
Powers and transparency letter secrets

Guards and safety
Training and self-regulatory happenings

Gatherings
Happy and interesting outdoor cinematic

Love and couples
Any and all forms legitimately

Travel or mobility
Portals and aeroplanes, trains, cars, buses, horses

Traditions
Dance and self-expression creative energy

Skills and trades
Varied and many guilds and unions

Discussions
Daily practices and praying habits and rituals

Health and wellness
Care, compassion, and imagination

Children and youth
Free, contained, and loved

Naming rights
All children to have at least three names

Education
Lifelong learning and studies

Work and life
Personal yet specific with changes and transitions

Thoughts or philosophy
Being and living to potential

Tagline or brief
Niainans are... Love

A last note: What is interdependence?

Interdependence is the answer to everything. It is the way forward. The interconnectedness of all things speaks to the state of the world. It has to do with quantum entanglement. Reality in another sense.

The truth is, should I not find my way home, or learn to make a home wherever I am, the fate that befalls the Steppenwolf will fall on me too. Forever wandering the earth, rootless, homeless, and lost to others, who can never find me, don't see me, and will never understand me. That is the dark side of not attaining independence, the way it feels and seems to me.

Hermann Hesse wrote about truth, freedom and self-determination in *Steppenwolf*. I read this book when I was only seventeen, and I probably only understood half of it, but I loved it and can't wait to re-read it.

On the other hand, I could reverse the curse and create my own world, which only those on their own special missions might have access to. That world is Niaina. So that is what I will do. And make a home where I am. As the daughter of immigrants, I feel like I am just arriving.

As for Kalinska, the EU is already involved with this place. In terms of development, Europe has given millions of euros in the last two decades. For its sustainability and for its socio-economic development. This contribution has helped to ensure a good relationship and a form of cooperation.

Due to the war in Ukraine, many ties have had to be severed lately. This is beyond sad for me personally and for others. I still wish the Russian people well, and thanks to their protesting the war and objecting to it, I can only sympathise. And I hope that things change in the future. May a peace agreement soon be reached and this disaster of a war between Russia and Ukraine come to an end. May the force be with us all. And may we return to an interdependent order very soon.

Any number of scenarios could materialise when it comes to the situation in Ukraine. Perhaps restraint could be exercised on all sides, or a nuclear war could happen, a winner could emerge, or World War III could begin, or a local war could continue, or peace negotiations could start, or a stalemate could happen, or further conflicts could arise, or rebel groups could form, or an energy war could erupt, or change could happen, or a natural disaster could strike, or a cooperation zone could be created, or the war could spread to Europe, or an internal uprising and a revolution could happen.

Europe is possibly on the brink of war. The avoidance of a nuclear war or any war that is spreading to Europe is a clear and present danger. We all need to do our bit to ensure that the best of communications, possible cooperation, and peace talks can take place. Whether it means praying, writing, making music, singing, protesting, participating, or defending what is yours, whatever your role, think about choices, life, and everything else.

Michelle Obama spoke of self-confidence, courage and how it can be contagious, in her book *Becoming*.

Upon reflection, I realized that I was probably just trying to create my own and other worlds in order to escape potential wars. Perhaps with courage and determination, we can face the challenges of the present time. And make interdependence and peace happen.

Chapter 9
Space

At the end of it all, I just want to acknowledge the Americans' influence over my life with respect to some of their laws, such as the law Thomas Jefferson created on the 'pursuit of happiness'. I love that law. It's liberating, inspires hope, and speaks to personal fulfilment.

Of course, the laws are not always right such as in the case of apartheid in South Africa. Without the struggle, change would not have been possible. In such instances where things are obviously wrong and hurtful to people, the laws need to be changed. An example of that in the world today is that there are still many countries with anti-gay legislation, and that needs to change, in my view. Also, laws that promote the rights of women need to come to the fore and be prioritised. Children's rights are crucial too. There needs to be space for co-existence and space for happiness. South Africa now has one of the best constitutions in the world. It was written and conceptualized by Albie Sachs. I hope others copy this brilliant work.

During apartheid, many people were hurt by an unjust system and individuals who exploited and used this system. To add insult to injury, there were massacres such as the Sharpeville massacre. People protested against the system, at first at home, then on a global level. It is only because of this, the struggle, and global sanctions by the US especially, that the apartheid regime came to an end. Thanks to the incoming leadership, a peaceful process was possible in the handover of power.

Nelson Rolihlahla Mandela became the first black president of South Africa. He took the mantle, but he did not reach this level on his own. He had many powerful and important colleagues in the struggle. And globally. Only the system had segregated people and made them live in different neighbourhoods as well as in homelands. Worst of all were the forced removals that happened, for example, in District Six and in Sophiatown. Interracial love was made illegal. Some people went into exile, and those who risked themselves often became political prisoners. Only some remained at home and continued their work in communities and in secret.

As resistance, in South Africa, the women's march of 1956 protested apartheid's pass laws and presented a petition to the government at the time. The march was led by Lilian Ngoyi, Sophia Williams Debruyn, Rahima Moosa, and Helen Joseph. This was a moment in history.

Nelson Mandela famously spoke of how important is is to make a difference in other people's lives.

Today, the people live in peace in South Africa, although global tensions are increasingly putting pressure on this fragile new democracy. As well as local challenges to the leadership and the system. The fight for a better life is far from over. And the gap between the rich and the poor is still overwhelming, even though a buoyant middle class is now in place. On the one hand, South Africa thrives; on the other, it struggles to survive. So poverty, corruption, and energy are huge challenges that need to be addressed. The history of the trade unions is well known, and they formed a critical part in the fight against apartheid. Dialogues can help address today's challenges, and many actions need to be taken. The people need to be more included in their own upliftment. And I am sure they will be. I have hope for the future.

But there is much healing still to be done. The Truth and Reconciliation Commission touched on issues. The archbishop Desmond Tutu and the panel observed the hearings and presided over the proceedings of the TRC. They did amazing work and brought into the open many things that happened during the dark times of apartheid. It shed some light on past events, but it was not enough. There is a further need for justice to take place. So that people can find it in themselves to eventually move on and find a healing space. A place of light.

On another note, another thing to mention here is that colonialism has wreaked havoc in Africa and elsewhere. At this time, it is important to create space and allow time for replenishment and regrowth. However, there is a new scramble for Africa with many new players. This is dangerous and opens the path for opportunists.

At this point, it would do us well to remember the Berlin Conference in Africa that happened in the 1800s, where countries in Europe co-determined the future map of Africa. This was largely so that they would not fight wars amongst each other on the continent. But they neglected to consult the people and leadership in Africa itself. So the maps were unethical and partially "wrong" and they cut off many people from one another.

This is, in some ways, still to be addressed, although the boundaries have been largely accepted and partially redrawn by now. In my view, there needs to be flexibility and room for change. We must allow for some future negotiations to take place and not enforce the status quo like *Hell Hath No Fury*. I do not wish for oppression in order to maintain peace. It isn't peace at all costs. It is peace upon agreements and space.

The Art of Peace was written by none other than Morihei Ueshiba, the founder of Aikido, a martial art and spiritual guide. In Aikido, you use the opponent's energy as well as your own energy. This combined force results in whatever it results in. Its shape is always unique. So it is on a case-by-case basis that we must confront the challenges ahead. The art of peace offers a non-violent approach to resolving conflicts and achieving lasting peace. I studied aikido for a year and a half, and it helped me a lot in my life.

Similarly, Mahatma Ghandi, who was born in South African, espoused a non-violent approach. He was a lawyer and an anti-colonial person who led India to its independence. He was unfortunately assassinated. But his legacy stands firm and strong.

Dr Martin Luther King also adopted the non-violent approach and called for an end to racism and for equal rights. His most famous speech was the "I have a dream" speech he made in Washington, D.C., in 1963. It was thanks to him and the civil rights movement that various laws were passed, including the Civil Rights Act and the Voting Act. Sadly, he was assassinated.

Another man who was famously assassinated was John F Kennedy, the much loved American president. He inspired a generation to take responsibility by taking political and social action. He fought for equal rights and an end to segregation in the US. He passed legislation to ensure access to public facilities, education, and the right to vote, amongst other things. He also spoke out on poverty and encouraged people to help one another. I have a photo of him and his wife, Jackie Kennedy, later Onassis, together. It's my ideal for a marriage.

A marriage with just enough space to create, and enough space to love one another. Now that's space. In 1969, when Neil Armstrong became the first man to walk on the moon together with his colleague Edwin 'Buzz' Aldrin, he said that it was "one small step for man, one giant leap for mankind," and so it is with asking for space. It is a huge achievement to get things into balance, to create systems that work, and maintain ecosystems that flourish. I hope for peace and prosperity for all humankind. In other words, space.

And schizaffective persons need a lot of space. For me, it has to do with the liberation of the self, and others. With freedom from fears, hurt, and pain. And anything that threatens life. Space to be me, myself, and I. And for others to be themselves. Space for independence and interdependence of the self, and for others. Space itself, space and land to exist and co-exist, space for development, for cities and townships and suburbs, and for smallholdings and farms. And space for creativity, playfulness, and fun. Space for intersections, crossroads, and the in between. Both mental and physical, real and imagined, past, present, and future times. That is more space.

A poem on space

>I would like to invoke for my family relatives
>Friends, colleagues, and fellow humans
>Their rights to:

>The pursuit of happiness
>Freedom of association
>And liberty and equality, and openness
>As well as a place called home.

>We denounce apartheid
>And acknowledge the Holocaust

The pain of slavery and colonialism
Also, any human rights abuses
And wars and conflicts
Of the present time.

I further hereby request
A return to peace times
And a right to protest and live on
And no further support of any wars
Whatsoever.

Reaffirming the constitution
And the laws of the land
Bound by spirituality and our core beliefs
Of which there are many
And what differentiates us defines us
And strengthens us
Yet impacts our abilities.

Beyond it all, we see
With vision and clarity
The path ahead and present times
Challenges and growth to face together
With mental diversity.

Change is inevitable
And we welcome more decisions
More hope, humbleness and better health
As time heals old wounds
And we overcome racial divisions and gender discrimination.

Going towards the next iteration
Reaching another level
Acceptance of diverse identities and
Existence and manifestation
Of what is us.

Spoken from the heart
Looking into the darkest of times
And the lightest of paths
Finding the way.

Chapter 10
Last Words

It's funny, but people have to deal with the past, present, and future of the places they live in as well. So whilst I might have thought a lot about where we came from, I haven't yet spent enough time reflecting on what's happening in the here and now present times on the ground. And where am I? In South Africa, Cape Town, to be specific.

My love for South Africa is clear. Without becoming too nationalistic, I have always been available for participating in making the country work. Nelson Mandela, the former statesman and struggle icon, asked people whether they were contributing to country building often. He gave people a blank slate and a new dream to work with. Some are currently disillusioned. Others are working on ameliorating the concept and making adaptations to it to suit new circumstances and more challenges as they arise.

In South Africa, we have had to face the many challenges of corruption, the pandemic, energy issues, massive unemployment, and more. I have books staring at me, waiting to be read, as I am still playing catch up on the history of this country. I have got a copy of Nelson Mandela's biography, *Long Walk to Freedom* (which I am halfway through), Steve Biko's *I Write What I Like*, a book about Chris Hani, *A Life Too Short*, a book by Albert Luthuli, *Let My People Go* and a book by Sisonke Msimang, *Always Another Country,* about a woman living in exile for many years. So I feel the struggle is all around me. Also, a new history of South Africa is on my bookshelf. It's important to know I didn't take history lessons at school or varsity; I more concerned myself with art history and current affairs. I was more of a visual person and couldn't remember numbers or dates at all.

Of course, I am not on my own. Other people around me also have their stories and ancestry, and I can't wait to see how some turn out. And other coffee table books I have include the likes of *Nomad* by Sibella Court, *The Kinfolk Home*, a place called home, *Counter Currents* by Edgar Pieterse, and the *Atlas of Beauty*, as well as *A Woman's World* and other art books. Yes... Maybe it's more about my friends, though. And one I would like to mention in particular. A previous colleague and friend of mine, Thandi. I realised one day that she is the epitome of and at the centre of the arts world in Soweto. She is literally IT, and so are many of her friends. And the same thing is happening here in places like Langa. With acquaintances like Siya building up bicycle hubs or tech places. A township meets a city kind of vibe. Development on track and happening at a speed faster than lightning, with connections occurring across the city and across worlds where previously there were both visible and invisible boundaries.

Then, well, it's important to understand that District Six is still a gaping void in the cityscape. It's such a space with opportunities. I understand people are being compensated. I think there is a lot more to it. I would prefer the people from there to comment and to listen to their voices. Some spaces that could hold those voices are the district six museum, the Iziko galleries, the centre for African cities, the design indaba, and the Hassno platter d-school at the University of Cape Town, to name a few. So I know the city quite well; I even worked in the east city development district for a while. I sat at a rented desk and enjoyed walking around the city, drinking cups of coffee, and eating cheese and tomato toasties. So many great delis and eateries have sprung up all over the place, there is a definite feel of an inner city revival. Perhaps I am a bit older now, and looking to spend more time at wine farms and fancy places along the Atlantic seaboard. That is where I grew up, after all, and where I fit in mostly. But I also don't want to be known as a snob and am always open to many.

At this point, aside from pointing out obvious opportunities, for people from here and elsewhere, I would also like to take responsibility and extend my heartfelt sympathy to anyone who was injured by apartheid, victims and survivors, and other people simply trying to live. I apologise profoundly and am deeply sorry if any of my actions ever contributed to any hurt, pain, or suffering. I issue an apology without reservation.

As the movement, *Black Lives Matter* swept across the world coming from the US. I was totally into it at first though, I later realised I am politically more in the middle of the right-left spectrum and couldn't fully align with the left. At least, I took on some advice and thought about my life deeply. I made some more friends and immersed myself in cultural aspects that I might have missed if I hadn't been especially looking. And I agree that an end to racism would be a perfect finale.

As a previously labelled 'white' person, I had some advantages and privileges that weren't due to me or anyone during apartheid or apart hate. At least not over and above other people who all deserved the same or at least equal benefits. Having said that, maybe I was a bit different from the rest of the 'white' South Africans, having gone to a German international school in Cape Town, a development focused school that let people in. What is crucial in any system nowadays is that "all shall be equal before the law."

At the end of the day, I am not going to relabel myself. Even though I could. I could describe myself as 'white Asian' at this point on the basis of the recent DNA test I took to discover more about my ancestry. But it's all just labelling. Race can be seen as more of a social construct. It's about the meanings people ascribe to the groups. And the groups themselves.

I feel if anything, what's more appropriate and accurate is to use places of origin and to have at least four or five of those per person. So each person gets a unique formula based on their ancestry. It means we are all snowflakes, as individual as can be. So it's no longer about racial groups. But it's about us all being beautiful individuals. Probably each belonging to at least four or five places of origin ourselves. It's a question of mathematics at the end of the day. Where are we from? Where are we now? Where are we going. People want to go places, though.

Mobility and flexibility are key and need to be enabled in the present and in the future times. In past times, the pass laws prohibited freedom of movement for the majority of the South African population. That was a grave injustice. To be able to move freely is nothing to take for granted. Ultimately, it's about reaching a place that is more of a feeling though. Like a place of love. Inside and out.

So. Let's spend some time facing the challenge of racism head-on. The classification system in apartheid days was something else. I don't know how it worked. I just know it hurts many people. It was an outrageous offense. Especially tying people's rights to it.

In Nazi Germany, racial purity, whatever that was, was espoused and revered. They pushed an agenda of absolute hate. There need to be anti-hate laws and other laws in place to deal with crimes against humanity. Germany has had denazification in its constitution since its inception. So Nazism and Neo-Nazism are illegal and criminal. It is also just wrong and immoral. Also, the problems with white supremacy require attention to this day.

I would like to look at the racial categories that exist in the world today. In South Africa, the categories were black, white, coloured, Asian, Indian, and others. In the US, the current categories on census surveys are: white, black or African American, Asian, American Indian and Alaska native, native Hawaiian and other Pacific Islander, or some other race. Additionally, people are allowed to report multiple races. In Germany today, people are still classed by places of origin in the census. In France, I think the government chose to be 'colour blind'. As we all should be. I am calling for that. With the consideration that reparations still need to happen. People who were disadvantaged in the past need to be paid what is due to them in compensation for losses and damages.

Nelson Mandela famously said that racism must be fought against and opposed in many ways. That is still relevant today.

What is racism? There are four levels of racism, according to the race forward model. Internalised racism is from within an individual, interpersonal racism happens between people; institutional racism occurs in institutions; and structural racism is racial bias within institutions and across society.

My feeling is that people should, as a next step, take out the racial categories. And by that, I mean we should no longer use them. Not any. Let's just throw them in the proverbial bin. It's a dangerous idea. Think about it. Instead of describing yourself according to one or multiple racial groups on a census questionnaire (like in the US), that question could be left out. Many people don't want to be labelled at all.

And in terms of addressing historical disadvantages, there

must be other ways to do that. Instead of using racial terms and qualifiers. Other terms could be used. The people who are ahead are the creators and developers of dating websites. There are no racial options. As this leads to negative discrimination. They are not using any racial qualifiers or descriptors.

It's a good idea. And everyone knows what happens to good ideas. They spread and multiply. They take hold and lay foundations. For new existences. Being open to the diversity of humans is love. In a nonracist society, all are at least colour-blind; in an anti-racist society, there is an awareness coupled with a desire for equality and a drive for equity. People actively speak out against and fight racism. Some are more inclined to be activists. Others just go along with the mainstream. In South Africa, we still have a long way to go.

There are many ways to combat racism and end discrimination, to prevent it from occurring in the first place. Anti-labelling is an aspect. And it starts with an education. As such, behaviours should be taught from an early age and attitudes reinforced in order to build a non-racial and anti-racist society. Similarly, gender discrimination needs to be addressed. Equality and liberty are key for a better, more fair, and more liveable world to emerge. This emergence is happening now. It is part of the shift in global energies.

Gender studies was my second major in my undergraduate degree in social science. Here's a brief synopsis of the different types of feminism and what they mean.

A feminist, as well as a humanist, can be a woman or a man whose beliefs and behaviours are based on accepting the underlying human equality of all people. Feminism is a political movement that helps to address inequalities. Strategies for social change are different. The main types of feminism are radical,

Marxist, liberal, and difference. Black feminism is about the experiences of black women and understanding their position in relation to racism, sexism, classism, and social and political identities. And then, indigenous feminism focuses on decolonization, indigenous sovereignty, and human rights for indigenous women and their families.

Postmodern feminists present an analysis of what led to gender inequality in society. Postmodern feminists promote equality of gender by supporting multiple discourses, and deconstructing texts, and promoting subjectivity. Then there are female millennials—women born between 1980 and 1995—who represent a significant new generation with unique voices of their own.

And there are various men's movements, which I honestly don't know that much about. I would guess that they are interested in rights around fathering and other men-specific issues. I am interested to learn more about these movements. We can all fight for mainstreaming inclusivity, diversity, and equality. We can ask for another world in many ways.

What is of great significance are the planetary energies of the moment. I have created seven energies to describe what is happening in the world right now. These illuminate what is going on. What interesting energies are circulating on the planet? They range from post-Nazism to post-colonialism, from post-apartheid to post-poverty, from post-slavery to post-religious, to post-generation X. Each energy is described using key words to draw a picture of the energy.

The planetary energies are the energies of our time. They shape us, they define us, they are a part of society, and they are the currents that run through. They are both responses to major events in history and also based on the struggles of many people and societies. Our cultures are defined by such undercurrents. We can harness the energies, and ride the waves they create. Or we can channel the energies in other ways.

Climate change and the need for sustainability are ongoing events. More and more natural disasters are happening. People all over the world are suffering. To be silent on this is close to criminal. When you can choose to be an activist or an actor making a difference. This runs through all the energies in different ways and with many different focus areas. Ecofeminism uses the basics of feminism, and combines this with a view of the world that respects ecology, holistic connections, intuition, and collaboration.

Whilst I haven't studied the history of slavery and don't know too much about it, I need to mention it here. From the blogs I have read and podcasts I have listened to, it seems to be the case that conducting slavery was all about families. Holding anyone accountable would therefore have to go back to the traders and the slave owners. It was less about countries, although those are also to blame, and more about specific networks and families. So to protest and try to hold people accountable, we need to be tied to the networks of old. What's probably most interesting is studying the history and lives of the slaves, what became of them, their origins, and their paths. Again to hear the voices of the people speak. Of course, there is also the phenomenon of modern slavery, which is terrible, and many are working to put an end to this. You, too, can help end modern slavery through activism.

Another aspect of life that is getting more attention at this point in history is mental health. As more people speak out and get candid about the state of their mental health and wellness. Some are brave enough to discuss their own mental illness in public. There is more activism on this than ever before.

All kinds of activism help to change the world, to push forward ideas, and to make things happen. They create space. For growth, and for humanity.

In the book *Power and Love*, the author Adam Kahane points out how love without power is sappy and sweet. And power without love is too strong and forceful. It is all about balancing the two. Plus, not forgetting about a healthy infusion of knowledge. That is what I wish for South Africa. For it to become a happy place. A prosperous and peaceful place free of negative and blocking energies. In the next chapters, I explore both power and love.

Planetary energies

Energies 1
Post Nazism
Way – Freedom, social, democracy, constitution denazification, Holocaust education, mental health, gender equality, family health and wellness, power with love, peace energy, and renewables human futures

Energies 2
Post Colonialism
Way – Independence, racial equity, democracy, autonomy, and multilateralism partnerships interdependence physical health and wellness back to the future gender existences sustainability afro futurism

Energies 3

Post-Apartheid

Way – Struggle peaceful transition, democracy, antiracism, social and economic liberty, and equality economic restructuring; production capabilities creative economy gender identities interracial relationships, Ubuntu ecology futurism diversity

Energies 4
Post Poverty

Way – Elevation to middle class beyond class system development; rich and poor beyond hunger; living well beyond sickness live healthy energy renewables agriculture diversification complex business trade sports and culture gender creativity, sustainability, love African futures

Energies 5
Post Slavery

Way – Freedom declaration abolition of slavery, old and modern working conditions, work and love, self-determination rights, life commitments, relationships, ownership and reparations love and black empowerment languages origins history, connectivity, ancestors, gender fluidity American futures

Energies 6
Post Religious

Way – Humanism return to pagan eco spiritual indigenous nature also regulation through Illuminati interventions, religion with balance more complexity and fluidity possibilities to change adaptations complex interfaith gay and lesbian marriages mental health, faith, and futures

Energies 7
Post Generation X
Way – Millenials Gen Z queer identities gender diversity multiracial complexities next-level humans into the future intergenerational power and love way forward youth life voices of today listening climate change activism gender futures and mental futures

Social identity markers:

    Age / generation
    National origin / where born and raised
    First language and languages spoken
    Physical, emotional, and developmental ability
    Religion and spiritual affiliation
    Educational background
    Family structure
    Citizenship status
    Race and physical traits
    Ethnicity, culture and customs
    Socioeconomic class and income
    Gender
    Sexual identity
    Mental health, health and wellness
    Physical abilities
    Consumer and brand personality
    Relationships and connection points
    Work status and career
    Politics and mind set

A poem on identity. Just a minute.

I don't know what we are or what I am, although, maybe I do, humans. At first, I thought I was nothing, then something, then a child of gods, then I was labelled 'white', eventually I arrived at previously 'white', then I realised I am beyond 'white', and beyond tribalism, with my hybrid identity, and I have arrived at nothing, at I don't really care, but I do, I think I am just diverse, but most of all, so is everybody else, if you look closely enough, but maybe blur that vision a bit, take a step back, look again, close your eyes, feel the spirit, your own, and others as well, before making any judgements, decisions, or taking actions, then also appreciate the uniqueness and the brilliance of individuals, in their collective identity, and on their own, together, and alone. Also, appreciate health and wellness, the wholeness and glory of your own body, the perfection of your vision, the ability to see, listen, hear, feel, understand, and learn with a sensory comprehension of the world and a lens on history, a spot of culture, and an open space, until you break through the complexities and see with extrasensory perception especially, internal vision, fanning out into the universe, its multitude of realities, and its quantum dynamics, and then come back and sit still, breathing and exhaling for a minute, of time, which belongs to no one.

Chapter 11
Power

Many living with schizophrenia or schizaffective disorder (which additionally includes depression) might feel that they have extraordinary powers and interesting insights. They might have access to alternative channels that regular humans do not typically use or subscribe to. Often, schizaffective persons hear voices talking to them, which might be coming from inside or outside of their own heads. If ever in such a position, it is important not to be scared and to engage and make friends with the voices, as they are clearly trying to tell you something. The more voices, the more overwhelming the experience might be. Therefore, many schizaffective persons try to shield themselves from overly loud and busy environments. It is best for them to live in quieter spaces and with less noise around them. However, there might be some truth to the idea that we or they have alternative insights. They might be able to access the Ethernet or alternate sources of information and indeed come up with new ideas and insights. Why not?

But sadly, most are dismissed and not regarded as the next-level communicators of collaborative intelligence. As for myself, I am happy to tell people about the results of my personality profile, which indicated that I am a 'special advisor'. That made me happy, and gave me space for marketing myself as a person with insights and relative powers.

There is so much to say about power. Great power should be tempered with wisdom, with love, with generosity, and with benevolence. Many in power go mad. It is unfortunate. In the future, those in power should have to pass mental health tests regularly. In order to stay in their positions or to hand over to successors or other suitable candidates. Sometimes it would simply be wise for some to take a much needed break and rest for a few months before returning to positions of power.

In terms of systems, personally, I believe in a social or liberal democracy. And in the separation of powers such as the judiciary, the legislature, and the executive. This is to protect all involved and to ensure a state and governance that is fair, just, and delivers. I think it's important to respect those willing to take on responsibilities, but also to provide space for those who wish to protest or provide alternative answers to the challenges at hand.

It's possible to discuss this for a lifetime.

If I had any powers, I would start with clarity of mind, and with love, and turn my attention towards the following:

On the system: always prepare for changes and challenges and create a rewards-based system. That is to say, a system based less on punishments, and more on rewards for good and lawful behaviours. Set, reset, and change the agendas from time to time, shifting the focus and allowing for flexibility and changes.

On reparations: there are many reparations that need to be done to balance the world. For example, reparations for slavery in the US by the US, whereby they should ensure families issue public apologies and take responsibility for what happened in the past. Reparations for colonialism should also be on the cards, for colonialism from Europe and the UK to Africa and elsewhere.

On trade: regular trade and investments should continue and continue to flourish. The stock exchanges could become stronger and more powerful. Changes and innovations in the monetary system should be observed and planned for. Fair trade for all.

On participation: more power could be given to the people through polls, referendums, and public participation. Tolerance and integration could be encouraged and promoted through incentives and campaigns in various countries. Always move people beyond their own identities and towards connections with others.

On climate change: many organisations and climate change initiatives need help, and natural disaster precautions and disaster prevention need to be better managed globally.

On health: those living with disabilities and illnesses could use additional assistance, and healthy lifestyles could be promoted. Those living with HIV/ AIDS and other issues would be able to live with dignity. The mental and the gifted should be supported through better laws, medication, and support programmes.

On indigenous peoples: there should be support for indigenous people with financial assistance grants and programmes. Support the global indigenous council to resurrect itself and come back into being, also promote mainstreaming. And first nation's status should be given to the indigenous Khoisan in South Africa.

On education: ameliorate the education system and start practical programmes and skills trainings for colleges and schools for artisans and for those with technical skills.

On peace: in Europe, the war in Ukraine should be ended and peace with Russia should be brokered. Transnational relationships would be restored. In Africa, peace between Ethiopia and Tigray should be ensured with peacekeeping forces. In Russia, interdependence for Kalinska with the European

Union should be guaranteed. In the Middle East, Israel and Palestine should reach an agreement and find the way towards peace. Syria should be further assisted in terms of refugees and the resettlement of people. Yemen should be helped. Many other countries in need of peacekeeping forces should be assisted.

On justice: military rapes and citizen rapes should be dealt with under the law and also privately. The legalisation of prostitution should be considered, or at least the decriminalisation of sex work.

On drugs and illegal substances: the drugs world should open up and legalisation of mid-class drugs, including weed, cannabis, and mushrooms should be allowed. The more natural things should not be criminalised. More medical research needed, and legalisation of micro dosing for war vets and others with trauma and PTSD. Therefore, allow for limited experimentation with clean synthetic drugs like LSD and ecstasy without criminalising. Continue to go against cocaine, opioids with the law, the police, and international networks.

On human trafficking: ensure that protections are in place and that human and sex trafficking is forbidden and fought against with the police, international networks, and society.

On the police and law enforcement: provide training and support to the police system and persons plus benefits and recognition.

On the medical world: ensure more medical trainings and support for workers, nurses, and doctors required, including spiritual guidance and help should be made available. Distribute medications where required through clinics and health systems.

On religion: all religions should be allowed to have a religious base with religious freedoms guaranteed and people allowed to practise their religions.

On genocides: immediate interventions in stopping genocides, massacres, and other types of killing of people, like ethnic cleansing, would be made possible.

On leadership: interruptions of leadership going bad or corrupt and regular changes in leadership and constant handovers would be allowed.

On refugees and migration: there should be better treatment of migrants, e.g., when entering Europe from Africa and at the US borders. Emphasis on flow and reception.

On futures thinking: an inclusive vision of African futures in Africa, more like Ubuntu futurism, should be made popular and be well known. In South Africa, the politics of the centre, both left and right, need to be strengthened and supported.

On corruption: anti-corruption should be promoted, and spending money wisely, financial acumen in budgets. Reward those going to work being productive and creative with opportunities.

On the social: those staying at home to be parents, whether male or female, should be assisted, fathering and mothering promoted, and caregivers given benefits and money.

On standard of living: it should be made possible to attain a reasonable standard of living for all, in South Africa and globally. To live well beyond the survival breadline yet within sustainable means and with values.

On mobility and movement: more travel should be possible, and experiences and sharing in other cultures. Cultural exchanges should be made possible.

On international security: work with anti-terrorism, and stop the growth of extremist and fundamentalist groups and individuals. Work against hate groups of any kind.

On international relations: work with all countries. Work also with the Far East, including China and Japan, and Southeast Asia, the Asian countries, and the G7, the G20, and the BRICS: Brazil, Russia, India, China, and South Africa. Continue to uphold and strengthen ties to Africa and Europe and various cities globally.

On development: give aid and development money to those who need support and other forms of love and opportunities.

On life and happiness: build some fresh additional temporary things, especially in established cities and old towns, to create fresh energy on top of existing things. Also temporary installations for new energies to flow.

On the UK: continue to validate the English system and the Commonwealth. Also, send love to the Irish and help them achieve lasting peace and remain part of the EU.

On survivors: continue to respect and pay tribute to the Holocaust survivors of Nazism and National Socialism.

On other survivors: pay tribute to the victims of Stalinism and other isms. Remember the Holodomor in Ukraine and ensure it never happens again anywhere. Stop famine and starvation in Somalia and the Horn of Africa, as well as elsewhere. Assist in the prevention of coups, e.g., in West Africa and military takeovers, e.g., in Myanmar.

On nature. Create more corridors for wild animals and spaces for conservation and wildlife. Rewilding nature allows for healing.

On technology: create tech spaces and a hi-tech culture everywhere intelligent life is possible, e.g., in Baltic countries like Estonia.

On energy: fix all energy issues and ensure and maintain a good energy supply. Balance the use of energy and reward energy and water saving behaviours. Create complex energy systems, including renewable energy systems, and ensure sustainability.

On water: protect water and let it flow through rivers and aquifers and as groundwater.

On relationships: protect true love, and others relationships and marriages and validate socially. Through the social compact. Allow for marriages and partnerships of all types of persons except not for children. Support family's creation and continuation in a positive way, allowing for changes, flexibility, and divorces as well as new marriages.

On food: ensure complex food systems exist and that there is space for artisans, chefs, and food lovers. Create agricultural systems that are more diverse, bio-friendly, small, and medium sized. Promote less meat and more vegetarian options for all; no big factory farming.

On transport: create mobility and transport systems that are compatible with environments and surroundings, and flexible and eco safe.

On mining: close mining of some minerals and metals, especially where conflict is involved. Ensure if mining is allowed that there is no blood involved, i.e., conflict-free and slave and child labour free.

On labour: stop modern slavery in all its forms and guises. And ensure good working conditions for those in jobs, no matter how temporary. Create more job opportunities for all levels. And respect holidays, religious ceremonies, and indigenous belief systems.

On reproductive rights: allow for reproductive rights, including abortion rights and practices, respect the choices of all women.

On LGBTQIA+: challenge all non-LGBTQIA+ countries on their legal systems and unfriendly, intolerant laws. LGBTQIA+ should be legal globally and gender-neutral pronouns used and passports offering a third option should be available.

On children: respect children's rights and give a voice to listen to them, hear them speak. Love and give opportunities to children, schools, and networks that support children.

On racism: work with anti-racism and equality campaigns and movements and promote diversity and women's rights. Balance power with love, respect, and trust. Continue to promote and endorse interracial and international love.

On professions: promote professions like doctors, lawyers, engineers, psychologists, and others.

On de-colonisation: connect more to Africa in various ways through friendships and in other supportive ways and assist in de-colonisation processes.

On the arts: appreciate, cultivate, and trust in all kinds of arts including art, music, dance performances, and so on. Give space to people to flourish, develop, and grow as human beings.

On the criminal justice system: only punish those who interfere with others life ambitions and plans and are criminals in a just and fair manner within the framework of the law. The law should be applied fairly and equally at all times. The prison system should be revised and buildings adapted. Gangs should be addressed by creating paths out and into alternative futures. The death penalty should be abolished. Rights to criminals should be granted, as in fair trials, privacy allowed and protections for all persons in place.

On vigilantism: ensure no stoning and mutilations of other persons or other outmoded vigilante practises; no mobbing or false accusations should be allowed. No vigilantism.

On animal rights: ensure respect for animal rights, and animal souls should be enshrined in the constitution. The recognition of the spirit or soul is important in granting these rights.

On languages: guarantee a love for languages and common languages, as agreed upon by the people and governments, should be welcomed.

On housing: create more social housing should be made available, with larger spaces (min: 100m2) available.

On cities: create better cities, and even new ones or extensions and add-ons.

On the ports: keep ports open and keep them professionally run and maintained. Continue with containers and shipping international business practices.

On black empowerment: assist justice and equity to come about in general, with love and balance, and with temperance and prudence.

On business: support small businesses and start-ups and accelerate and promote growth and opportunities.

On education: give money to schools to be better and more interesting and to connect technologies. Ensure networks of teachers that are capable, well-educated, and professional.

On faith: respect all faiths and belief systems, yet with adaptations possible, and living by and adhering to the constitution of the land.

On freedom of speech: be allowed to write what we like, as Steve Biko, the struggle icon, said, but without any hate speech or incriminating words.

On war vets: support war vets more with financial assistance in general globally. And continue to promote anti-apartheid messaging and the struggle for freedom, independence, and rights.

On cooperation: promote interdependence, multilateralism, and cooperation amongst nations, and build regions, regional thinking, and collaborations from time to time.

On leadership: celebrate past leaders and cultivate future ones. Make sure succession planning is in place. Always promote and listen to expertise and use consultants for direction, yet make your own decisions as leaders do.

On the elderly: trust and respect the elderly and support care for the aged as well.

On neighbourliness: assist those in and from any neighbouring countries, e.g., Zimbabwe, with financial aid, food aid, and other opportunities, assist in rebuilding the country.

On learning: continue with lifelong learning at all times through books, conversations, and other ways of accepting learning and life lessons. We should take notes on everything, draw maps, charts, diagrams, and stay ahead of changes, e.g., to the money systems or to climate change. We could, imagine the future all the time, past and present, and draw it make it visual and accessible for others to understand.

On men's rights: men's rights need to be promoted. For example, take special leave when becoming a new father.

On women's rights: women's rights need to be protected and ensured. For example, the right to equal pay is important.

On gender: trans and intersex rights need to be guaranteed. And provisions for a third category made available in legal documents such as passports, on ID cards, and drivers licenses.

So, in summary, attention would need to be given to many different topics. These would all be on the agenda. Thinking about things is not enough, actually doing what needs to be done is essential. The future needs to be anticipated and planned for as well.

Thank goodness also for human rights. Human rights, the rights for all human beings, e.g., the right to life and liberty, freedom from slavery, freedom of opinion and expression, the right to work and education, and many more.

Of course, many believe that power should go to the people, and so do I. However, there needs to be good leadership in place – leaders that can represent the people and that are chosen by the people as well. In South Africa, you say "amandla" and the response is "awethu" which means as much as power to the people. This was a huge part of the struggle against apartheid. Having a voice and the ability to participate as a citizen, like through participatory practises, is really important. At this point, I want to say thank you to all the people who struggled for creating the world we live in today in South Africa. Thank you for liberating the people. And for finding leaders to lead the way.

One of the key things about leaders is their ability to resolve past issues and conflicts, to address present challenges, and to plan ahead for the future and potential events and occurrences.

Antoine de Saint-Exupery reflected on the future in *The Little Prince* and the ability to enable it. It's important to be able to make it happen.

I was in Paris on Bastille Day once, and I celebrated "Liberté, Égalité, Fraternité." I totally believe in those ideas. I have also been to the love parade in Berlin and danced away the night. Not on my own, of course, but with dear friends. I have been to many themed MCQP parties in Cape Town in my more hedonistic youthful days. In Joburg, I went to poetry nights and danced in Brixton. In London, I went to mass and other places. I did all of that. That was in my power.

Also, I have done my fair share of activism. I was an activist for HIV/AIDS and for improving access to medicines. That was critically important many years ago. I have made a difference as a volunteer in the arts and in working with homeless children. It is in anyone's power to participate and make a contribution towards society. There is much space for that.

If leaders are not good, they are often deposed. Such is the case with revolutions. The only revolution I ever participated in was the Arab Spring, and all I was doing was watching it happen online. When the people deposed the president, Hosni Mubarak. The internet had been shut down, and some individuals made alternative modes of communication accessible to the public. The revolution went ahead. It was unstoppable. What an energy.

Revolutions helped get the people to where they are today, in France and modern-day Russia. I don't know much about the French Revolution, but it sounds like it was an interesting time in history. In Russia, the czars are still recovering from a family execution that happened many years ago. Recently, a czars wedding was held and validated by the orthodox Christian church. No matter what side you might think you are on, I hope that in the end, love always wins – the love of a couple, and the love for a people.

The thing is that lasting change doesn't always happen that quickly or suddenly. Percentage variation change indicates how comfortable or uncomfortable we are with change. Lasting change requires visionary and powerful leadership supported by networks.

My aunt Isabel gave me some interesting books to read. She chose them carefully. One was Pope Joan. The story is that for a few days there was a female pope once. The book describes the process of a new pope coming into being. It's a fascinating process. The choice of the person is significant. The voting for the pope. Smoke signals are used to signify success in the papal election. Thank goodness elections are a generally accepted thing in the world today.

And so, power is passed on from generation to generation, from person to person.

What I stand for:

Niaina (global super node)
People (can be great, love, or protest)
Anti-terrorism (London 2005) for sanity
Anti-gender based violence (no violence) for safety
Disability awareness (love) for health and mobility
Mental health (psychology)
Anti-racism (for diversity) for rights
Anti-sexism (gender studies) for equality
For sustainability (anti-climate change)
South African (Nelson Mandela and Struggle, ID)
And German (family, the Holocaust, and WW2)
For interdependence (bi and multi literalism agreements)
LGBTQIA+ (friendly, rights mainstreaming, sexuality)
Spiritual (many faiths and connectedness)
With the American (family, and development)
And global (trade and relationships)
Indigenous rights (dignity and life, mainstreaming)
Anti-apartheid (anywhere, SA)
Pagan (core underlying beliefs)
And Christian (habits rituals and traditions)
With the Jewish (family, rights)

Buddhist inspired (health and wellness)
Aikido (harmony, way of energy, peace)
African spiritualties (all Ubuntu)
Anti-war and conflict (for peace, and resolutions)
Personalism (MLK, human dignity social)
Humanism (human development, greater good ethical behaviour)
Existentialism (Franklin, hope and life)
Independence (autonomy, decision making)
Health and wellness (staying well)
Heritage (various aspects)
Location (Cape Town, plus, Hamburg)
Energy (life forces)
Hybrid (identities, futures)
Nature (and wild animals)
Good governance (politics, leadership)
Anti-expulsions (for refugees)
Anti-genocide (anywhere)
Anti-Nazism (for a modern Germany)
Anti-Stalinism (for Russia)
Post-soviet (a more integrated life)
For peace (for Ukraine)
Anti-colonialism (Africa especially)
Anti-slavery (global and modern)
Against polarisation (for diversity, politics)
For the pursuit of happiness (as in US)
For poetry (writings)
For art (visual, other)
For music (healing, life, energy, vibrations)
For science (learning)
For education (hope for the future)

For artificial intelligence (AI)
For technology (intelligent)
For basic needs met (food, shelter)
For family (own, others)
For social rights (social democracy)
For energy (for all)
For integral thinking (for life)
For love (for all)

Protected by the highest laws
Tiago (May God protect)

Chapter 12
Love

Oh, but what is love. Many philosophers, thinkers, writers, and psychologists have written about love. Here are thought starters on love from some of the world's greatest thinkers.

Erich Fromm says in *The Art of Loving* that love is a universal orientation towards others that promotes autonomy and mutual respect for humanity. Love is based on care, responsibility, respect, and knowledge. This means people would have to know each other in order to love each other. And as such, this is an expansion on romantic love.

Immanuel Kant believed in freedom of thought. He introduced the concepts of logical, practical, and transcendental freedom, as well as freedom of choice. He thought humans should have the right to dignity and respect. Love is therefore also a choice.

Frantz Fanon wrote on de-colonial love, and he fought for the independence of Algeria. He saw colonialism as violent and dominating. He wanted a world free of oppression and dominance over people. Black consciousness as a form of self-liberation. And a way to move away from self-harming and towards self-affirming beliefs. The self is seen as a potential catalyst for socio-political change.

Simone de Beauvoir was a feminist whose writings impacted second wave feminism. She emphasised that women need to participate in the world in a similar way as men. On romantic love, she said that a person is dependent on another and the self is subject to another. She was in a relationship with Jean-Paul Sartre, the philosopher.

Toni Morrison was anti-slavery and wrote in her novel, *Beloved* that the past should not be an impediment to the present. Thus allowing people to move on from the past and heal. On love, she said that love is not better than the lover. As such, wicked people love wickedly, and so on. Love is for the lover to give. She gave America a chance to rise above the past and become a modern state.

Bell Hooks commented that, in modern times, love is an overused word. She sees love as an action and suggests ways to improve love between people in her book, *All about Love: New Visions*. She notes that power discrepancies between men and women remain an issue, and expectations are different for men and for women.

Robert Sternberg, the psychologist, postulated that the three components of love are intimacy, passion, and commitment. The first is a feeling of attachment, and connectedness. Passion is connected to sexual intimacy and attraction. Commitment is the bond that holds it all together.

Richard Von Krafft-Ebing identified five types of love: true love, sentimental love, platonic love, friendship, and sensual love. These surely all exist, and we will hopefully experience them over the course of a lifetime.

Lastly, the American Psychological Association (APA) defines love as a "complex emotion involving strong feelings of affection and tenderness" for a person.

My definition of love is simple. To love is to care. To love is to know someone. To love is to be there for someone. To love is to have deep affection. Sometimes it comes with passion. That is romantic love. But one also needs to have love for humanity, especially to be a good leader, any kind of leader, or even just to be a person – part of a society. The social fabric depends on it. Love matters.

I also think that to be able to love others, we need to have a certain reasonable amount of self-love. And respect for ourselves as well as our hopes, dreams, and aspirations for our lives, and the lives of others. I am going to practise self-care and self-love. As a schizaffective person. The meaning of this label remains highly elusive. In part, it indicates a person who might have hallucinations or delusions, be disconnected from reality or be highly confused and with mangled speech patterns. This might be the state of a person during an episode. In order to avoid such occurrences and events and prevent them from happening, it is best for a schizaffective person to regularly take medication and stay sane enough to participate in the world. As I do. And I have promised to love myself enough.

In the future, perhaps there will be an understanding of schizophrenia and schizaffective disorder, as well as other mental conditions, as more temporary, as nothing but a passing phase, as events that come and go, and not as lifelong chronic conditions. However, this would also depend on the recovery a person has made, whether it was partial or complete, and whether the person affected is living at a level comparable to that of regular individuals. That would be love.

Love is... inclusive, giving, tolerant, open, existential, person-centred, interactive, and potentially LGBTQIA+, and so on.

In terms of my sexual orientation, I would probably describe myself as mostly straight. I haven't yet had the good fortune of dating a woman, but I would possibly be open to that as well. My experiences in this life have been with men. I think sexuality is a great gift, and I think we should treasure it. Humans were not made only for procreation but also to experience pleasure. I have a great book about sextrology, which explains a lot about personality and style according to the zodiac signs. It's quite a serious and interesting read. Our sexualities are something we should appreciate.

I hope for an open society, one where we can all live together in peace and not be in situations of intimidation or live with violence. I am against gender-based violence, GBV, or intimate partner violence. It is a heart-breaking thing, and it should not be taken lightly or ignored. The Catholic approach is best, if s/he hits you even once; it's best to leave that relationship immediately. Love should never hurt.

Love should bring out the best in two people, help them grow to their full potential, heal wounds where necessary, and open up new possibilities. A life together should always add up to more. Of course, it's not always love; sometimes two people just like each other, care for each other, want to be passionate together, or are madly infatuated with each other. Temporary connections are valuable too, no matter how short-lived, and can be just as deep as longer-term relationships.

What else do I know about love? Well, of course, there is parental love and family love too. I don't take that for granted, and I work on these relationships. I have even worked on them in therapy and am this year doing a course on family systems as part of an honours degree in psychology. I love psychology, and I think it's my calling in life. I feel lucky to know that. Understanding people, relationships, behaviours, and life is my passion. I wish for all people to find a purpose in life.

Last but not least, my tarot cards, as read by a number of people, including myself, have always revealed that I would find true love in this life. And I think I have found it. I am deeply in love with a man. It fills me with gratitude, contentment, happiness, and an all-pervasive sense of love. It gives me a glow, and a sense that the world is a great place to be in. I hope for this man that he might live his best life, and I would love to be the person he chooses to do this together with. I just don't know yet, and the not knowing, whilst frustrating, also opens up a space of exploration, hope, and exhilaration. I want nothing more than to be together with this person. I am a woman in love.

I have great respect for tarot card readers, mind readers, seers, and other mentally talented people. There are many kinds around, and it continues to surprise me, what possibilities there are. It makes me think also of the Roma and the Sinti, many of whom were said to possess unique talents of the mind. Unfortunately, they were another target group during the Nazi period, and National Socialism almost wiped out this community in Europe. I visited the Roma and Sinti Memorial in Berlin, a shallow round pond with many triangular stones in it to acknowledge individuals. It also speaks to clarity, and sometimes the pool is crystal clear, on other days, it looks muddy, murky, grey, and reflecting the mood of the day and the skies above.

As a last word, mental health is something to value, and to continuously work on. We all should do this: monitor ourselves, look out for our own wellbeing, and practise self-care and self-love as well. There are many kinds of mental states and many mental illnesses that can trouble individuals and even entire communities and plague societies. I think that there are different ages for mankind. We might be entering another age, an age that is more feminine. With a slight global shift towards the east, this is a possibility. As this is where that energy lies. That is my prediction.

Love for all people is something we can also practise. Getting to know many cultures is possible through exposure, through reading, listening, learning, traveling, and talking with many people. I hope to do a lot more of that in my life. So far, I have been lucky to have travelled to Argentina, South Africa, Namibia, Mozambique, Malawi, Mauritius, Australia, New Zealand, Malaysia, Indonesia, and most of Europe, including Great Britain, Germany, France, Spain, Italy, the Netherlands, Denmark, Sweden, Finland, Estonia, Latvia, and Russia. Each trip has left me totally inspired and with a sense of love for the world and its people. I like to think that I am open-minded.

I would like to travel a lot more. Preferably not on my own. For example, I would like to visit Botswana, Angola, Israel, India, Vietnam, Cambodia, China, Japan, Spain, Portugal, France, Bulgaria, Hungary, Italy, Brazil, Chile, Mexico, the USA, Canada, Egypt, Morocco, Algeria, Turkey, Germany, Tanzania, Kenya, Ethiopia, Mozambique, the UK, Scotland, Ireland, and Mauritius. It's a bit random, but most of those places I haven't been yet. Or would like to revisit.

A form of love is also sharing stories. For example, I met a guy in Geneva called Emile who was from Rwanda. One day, he sat me down and told me the whole story of the genocide that had happened there. It was in French, so I didn't understand all of it. But I could sense the emotions. I will remember that interaction forever, and I wish the people of Rwanda well.

I think that it will take a long time to heal the deep hurt that has been created by systems like apartheid in South Africa and ongoing racism in various countries. I hope people will choose the path of love, balanced with power. That is, I hope we or they will feel empowered and able to live our or their lives to the fullest potential. I believe in growth and in human development. In people unfolding themselves and discovering that layer after layer there is always more.

As a consequence, I love art and photography and have many other hobbies, such as walking, swimming, and listening to music, art, and creative writing. That too is energy – another kind of love. Something that gives you a sense of well-being and fulfilment. It can allow you to engage critically with topical issues and find an inner voice. To find connectedness, and to apply knowledge, and as an expression of feelings.

Therefore, to answer the question, love is… Perhaps in the shape of a flower. Maybe its shape shifts. It is a warm white light. It is whatever it is…

Love is also my cat, Misha. I have never felt such unconditional love, respect, and trust. As with this personage, this personality is noteworthy. He is part wild cat, part house cat, and makes beautiful sounds, quite unlike those of your regular house cat. He has protected me, loved me, and valued me unlike any other being. I have such a deep love for him; it's an unbreakable bond, between a human and an animal. To reiterate that, I think animals should have more rights in this world and be recognised as sentient beings with a spirit, a soul, or whatever you might believe in. At least believe in love.

At this last moment, I would like to thank my mother and my brother for all they have done for me in this life and for being who they are. They are truly special souls, and I love them very much. I haven't said it nearly enough.

In this life, I wish you love.

Signing off.
Hayley

What is true love?

True love is a gift.
It is acceptance.

It is freedom.
It is endless, and it goes through time.

True love is a rarity.
If you find it, never let it go.

It is a blessing.
Appreciate it.

It is liberation.
It is a wonderful thing.

It lifts the spirit.
It kindles the heart.

It is kindness.
True love unfolds.

Epilogue

Formula for life and survival

    Self-defence basics:
    Take from the energy of yourself and your opponent
    Act with ten times more force and energy
    With energy from within and without

    To deal with dark matter
    And dark energy and dark forces

        1. Block, e.g., a person
        2. Disrupt, e.g., a situation
        3. Diffuse, e.g., a bomb
        4. Develop, e.g., a place

    Return to the light
    Stay mentally strong and focused

    Talk against
    And keep your vision strong and bold
    Make it happen:
    Single-mindedly pursue
    Act from an internal locus of control

    Get to the point of survival

And thrive and prosper

Bring out people and the best in them
Reach human growth and potential

Love
Infused with power
Balanced with temperance and grace

Connect
Share visions and ideas
Network and give of your energy
And take from others

Remember
Find and seek out wisdom and happiness

Live